The Devil's Patch

The Hunt for the Foul Murderer of Ichabod Crane

Sleepy Hollow Horrors: Book Two

AUSTIN DRAGON

Published by Well-Tailored Books, California

The Devil's Patch / Sleepy Hollow Horrors (Book 2)

978-0-9909315-5-3 (hardcover)
978-0-9909315-4-6 (paperback)
978-0-9909315-3-9 (ebook)

http://www.austindragon.com

Book cover design by Erika Gizelle Santiago

Formatting by Polgarus Studio

Printed in the United States of America

Contents

Introduction

My part in this horrific affair began five years ago. My parents had learned of the death, indirectly through third parties, two years after the original event in, of all things, a ghost story, and inquired further. When I became aware of the tragedy, I took the inquiries upon myself until I came to know a man named Diedrich Knickerbocker. It was his last post, in our nearly one year correspondence, that not only gave the fullest account of the alleged circumstances of the original event, but also the surrounding background and details. It was that letter that precipitated my quest, which, unsurprisingly to all who know me, evolved into my current situation.

In the late autumn of 1790, Ichabod Crane, a well-likeable schoolmaster in the New England town of Sleepy Hollow, disappeared in body from the face of God's Earth. Folks say in whispers what they refused to say aloud—he was 'taken' by the chief spirit that haunted the Hollow—the Headless Horseman.

Aye, this Headless Horseman. Some say, this horseman was bewitched by a German warlock in the earliest days of colonial settlement. Some say, an ancient Indian chieftain and sorcerer held dark pow-wows on the very land that is the Hollow. The Horseman, who, as legend has it, had his head carried away by a cannonball in the War, haunted the Hollow's valley in his nightly quest for his head. This Horseman is a giant of a man—albeit headless—in black clothes and a massive cloak, sitting on a fearsome black horse. This Horseman chases his unfortunate mortal victim, rising in his stirrups to throw its dreadful pumpkin, then passes by like a whirlwind, and disappears into the night.

Aye, they would declare, the Headless Horseman of Sleepy Hollow.

I, however, believe in no such feeble supernatural tales, though the simple people of Sleepy Hollow regard them as unimpeachable certainties. However, the murder of a man, in all my considerable experience despite my youth in age, remains the province of other men of flesh and blood, and not ghosts and boogiemen. The Foul Murderer of Ichabod Crane is whom I seek. And when I find this man, without any hesitation to burden myself with any civilized reflections or academic considerations in 'seeking justice and not revenge,' all irrelevant to my purpose and irrelevant to my hunt, I shall kill this devil.

— Julian Crane, nephew of Ichabod Crane, 1800

Part I
The Hessian

"Hello, my name was Ichabod Crane. I'm dead."

His very eyes bulged from their sockets. His teeth jutted forward from his wide-open mouth, unable to scream. His ponytail flew and flapped behind his head, and his hands clutched his horse, Gunpowder, with inhuman strength borne out of the depths of panic.

Ichabod rode the horse out of Sleepy Hollow in the grips of incredible terror. The ground was ripped up with the terrible force of his horror-stricken horse as both man and beast disappeared into the night.

In close pursuit, the black goblin horse appeared with its huge, misshapen, towering rider—a glowing pumpkin already in the rider's hand. The rider had neither neck nor head on his shoulders. They raced after their prey like an unstoppable force.

It was a fall day in 1790, and it was Ichabod Crane's last night—last day—alive.

More Hollow Blood

"My name was Finn Shaunessy. I'm dead now."

It was a fall day in 1790 …

The Headless Horseman of Sleepy Hollow, the Headless Hessian, or simply, the Horseman. These were all the most common names for the demonic thing that reigned over the night in this haunted region of the Hudson River Valley, known as the Tappan Zee. All these names were written in the outer margins of the page.

The crude sketch was unmistakable. Shaunessy stared at it in his little journal with its well-worn, brown leather cover. He flipped through the pages of his detailed handwritten notes, and then paused to glance back at the sketch again. He closed it, bookmarking it with a folded letter.

"How reliable is the postal service in these parts?" he asked.

The general store was well-stocked with everything from dinnerware and glassware to woven clothes of varied colors, men's clothing and women's dresses, and fresh and dried vegetables. He was only interested in some buttons to patch up his extra shirt, candles, coffee, a few books, and some candy.

The storekeeper, a large man with red-freckled skin and a bushy red mustache, stopped his vigorous sweeping of the floor. He looked at the journal and letter in Shaunessy's hands.

"If you post it, it will get to the person you send it to. When? I couldn't say. Where's it going?"

"Manhattan."

The storekeeper nodded. "It will get there fine." He gestured with his hand to follow and walked to the front counter; leaning the broom against the wall.

Shaunessy joined him at the counter. He hesitated as he looked at the journal again.

"Changing your mind?" the storekeeper asked.

Shaunessy thought for a moment, then decided. "I'll send it. But I'll most likely get home before it arrives."

"I can package it for you, too."

"Thank you kindly."

The storekeeper moved to a shelf to grab the packing materials.

"Is there a local tavern you'd recommend?"

"Eating or drinking?"

"I'd like to do both."

"If you want a good meal, then I'll send you to one place. If it's to get drunk, then I'll send you someplace else."

"Drinking." Shaunessy looked down at his hands. "I may need a bit of extra courage tonight," he said, almost to himself.

"I won't tell you your business, sir, but normally when you need extra courage to do something, then you probably shouldn't do it."

Shaunessy chuckled. "I would have said no different to my own son. He's headstrong like me. No. I have to go through with it. It's the culmination of years of research and planning. I intend to be a famous man. I'm a writer by trade, and I have the story to make my historical travelogue so famous that it will only be surpassed by the Holy Bible in popularity."

"Famous, huh?" The storekeeper looked up at him for a second with a grin as he continued to package up the journal with a letter.

"I shall be the only man to come face-to-face with the Headless Horseman, himself, and live to tell the tale."

The storekeeper stopped wrapping and looked up, his mouth hanging open.

Tarry Town's main tavern was overflowing with rowdy patrons. Not a single man was without a drink in hand; some had a drink in each hand. Shaunessy, like every other customer who wanted to be served in the establishment, had to push his way through the crowd to the main bar and one of only two servers.

"What's your pleasure, sir?" the average-looking, dark-haired barman asked.

Shaunessy leaned forward on the bar, eyeing all the bottles in front of him.

"Quite a fine selection, sir. You have me stumped, and it's quite a feat to stump Finn Shaunessy when it comes to the drink. A fine selection you have. A very fine selection." Shaunessy covered his eyes with his open hand and then randomly pointed forward with his other hand. "That bottle." He peeked from behind his hand. "Start with that one. Line 'em up." He grabbed one of the empty glasses on the bar and turned to face the customers in the establishment, raising up the glass. "And line them up for everyone! Compliments of Finn Shaunessy!"

The tavern erupted in shouts of joy as men moved to the main bar.

"That's mighty generous of you, mister. The only other man in these parts as generous is Brom Bones."

"Who might he be?"

"Of late, the wealthiest man in these parts."

"Then there's no competition. I'm generous, not wealthy."

Men in the tavern approached him to give thanks. Finn got his first drink, and the barman emptied one bottle in glass after glass for each man, and then got another bottle to continue.

"Whereabouts are you from, Mr. Shaunessy?"

"Down by Manhattan, presently."

"Ah, I've been there. Family?"

"Lovely wife and a son who's growing into a fine man."

"What brings you here?" asked another man.

Finn Shaunessy began to laugh to himself. "Ghosts." He gulped down his second drink. He then turned to another man, seeing an untouched mug. Shaunessy grabbed the mug out of the man's hand.

"Ghosts?" the man asked.

Shaunessy began to drink again. "I've always wanted to see a ghost with my own eyes, and everyone in the last town told me that if that's what I'm beggin' to do, then this town is the place to go."

"Where did they tell you to go?"

"Sleepy Hollow."

"This is not Sleepy Hollow, mister. This is Tarry Town."

Shaunessy stopped drinking for a moment. "They told me the wrong place?"

"Not the wrong place. You're just two miles shy from the right place. It's the next town over."

Shaunessy smiled and started to drink from his glass again.

"But … why would you want to meet ghosts? People run from ghosts, not to them."

"I'm writing the official, accurate account of this region entitled, *The True Supernatural History of the Hudson Valley: Ghosts, Strange Happenings, and the Legend of Sleepy Hollow.*"

"What Legend are you speaking about, mister?"

"The Headless Horseman of Sleepy Hollow, of course," Shaunessy replied.

"Outsiders call it the Legend," one man said to another.

At first, the men surrounding him, sloshing back their drinks, paused. Was he playing a joke on all of them? After a moment or two, they realized he was serious.

"Is this you talking or the liquor, mister?"

Shaunessy laughed. "Good question. Probably more drink than me, at this point. But we both are saying the same thing."

"You're mad. You find the Horseman and you'll never be seen again," one man said.

"It finds you, and you'll never be seen again," said another man.

Shaunessy answered, "I doubt that. Many people have seen it, and they are still alive. Otherwise, there would be no Legend. In fact…"

"Because it was after someone else," a man interjected. "That's the only thing that saved their lives."

"What do you mean?" Shaunessy asked.

"It fixes on one man and ignores all others when it rides to attack," the man answered.

Shaunessy nodded. "I surmised the same thing, but…There are many accounts of sole riders, or sole travelers on foot, in its domain falling prey."

"But none of those accounts are true," the same man countered. "Any man by himself would be taken, and no one would ever know—unless there was another witness."

"You're very certain of it," Shaunessy noted.

The man was tall with a large mustache, stubble for a beard, and he wore a long tan coat that almost touched the ground. Shaunessy glimpsed a gun belt underneath.

"I'm a lawman," the man answered. "But not in these parts."

"What you're saying is that some of the ghost stories of the Horseman are true, and some are not."

"You can tell when a man has genuinely seen the Horseman with his own eyes and those who're just telling tales."

Shaunessy asked, "What's your name, sir?"

"Damian Marshal."

"Have you seen the Horseman, Mr. Marshal?"

The lawman paused as everyone in the tavern watched the exchange between the two men.

"I have."

A tipsy Shaunessy staggered out of the tavern arm-in-arm with a dozen other drunk men. All of them singing the same drinking song.

"Shaunessy, you are in no state to go looking for the Horseman," one man managed to say, slurring every other word. "You are in no state to ride your horse. You are in no state to walk in the road. You are in…" The man tripped over his own feet and fell face-first into the dirt. The crowd of men began laughing hysterically. A couple more men stumbled and fell to the ground, causing another outbreak of group laughter.

Shaunessy jumped up and down in place and then shook his head back and forth. "I'm going!"

"Going where, Shaunessy? To see the Horseman?"

"If I were doing that, I wouldn't be here the whole night drinking with you fine men. I'm going to bed."

The men laughed at him. "Courage has left you?" one man said.

"Not the courage. The warmth from my bones. It's too cold. I can only be brave on warmer nights, so I'll settle, figuratively and literally, on a warm bed instead."

Men began to laugh again.

"Where's my horse?" Shaunessy asked.

A few of the men grabbed him and walked him to the livery stables. Most of the men were local, so with the spectacle over; they began walking home, calling out goodbyes to their drinking friends.

Shaunessy saw his horse, ran to it, and hugged it. The laughs began again, and then intensified when he tried unsuccessfully to get on the horse.

"Shaunessy, you can't even mount your own horse. Walk the horse."

"Get me up. I'll manage."

Two men pushed him up, and finally Shaunessy managed to swing a leg over and get on. He grabbed the reins and sat up, somewhat straight, to move his horse out.

Men waved and called out goodbyes as he rode out and left them behind.

"Wait, wait," Shaunessy said to himself. "Where am I going?"

"Where do you want to go?" A sole man stood in the road with a lantern. His face was familiar.

"Well, not Sleepy Hollow. I shall save that for another day. Which way to the inn? I have a rendezvous with a warm bed and good sleep."

The man smiled. "The last inn on the way out of town?"

"Yes, sir."

Damian Marshal grabbed the reins of his horse and turned them around. He pointed down the road into the night. "There. And you'll need this." Marshal handed him the lantern. "Take mine."

"Thank you, fine sir." Shaunessy waved him a goodbye and rode out again.

Shaunessy galloped past a few men slowly walking down the road to their homes in Tarry Town. The center man held their only lantern.

"Isn't that the Shaunessy man?"

"Looks like him."

"Why is the fool riding into Sleepy Hollow on a cold, dark night like this?"

"He wants to trade in being drunk and foolish with being dead and foolish."

"Shouldn't we go after him?"

"It's his fortune to risk. It's cold. It's dark. There's not even a moon out. I gotta walk you two home and then get to mine. I'm tired. No. Let him go."

A shivering Shaunessy turned up his collar, trying to cover as much of the open skin on the back of his neck as possible. He could see his breath more and more as his horse galloped along. The lantern was a blessing as it brightened the way, but it was also a curse. His left hand was painfully numb from the cold and holding the lantern's shiny, metal handle.

He glanced back and then swung the lantern to the front of his face.

I heard something.

He turned back around and dug into his horse's sides with his boots. "Ya, boy. Move faster. Get us off this dark road and out of the cold. Why is it so cold all of a sudden?"

Shaunessy got quiet. He held his head down as his eyes darted around nervously. He jerked his entire torso to look back again. This time, he stopped the horse.

Something's following me.

"Who's back there?" he called out. "I am in no mood for pranks. Come out from back there."

It wasn't that the night was so dark. It was the rider behind him was so black. Shaunessy's eyes widened as the rider seemed to melt out of the darkness to meet the illumination from the lantern. Shaunessy froze at first, trying to make out what he was seeing. *The rider seemed to have no head.*

As it drew nearer, Shaunessy noticed the hugeness of the man on the jet-black horse. He guessed the man was almost seven feet if he were standing, outfitted in what appeared to be military dress of some kind and a billowing cloak. He stared at him for a long while when he glanced at the man's horse. *Impossible.* Its eyes stared back with a menacing gaze—eyes glowing a dull red. He could not be sure, but its mouth seemed to be filled with fanged teeth.

"Who are you?" Shaunessy asked with no sense of drunkenness. That state had left him.

The headless rider made no movement. It sat on its frightful horse facing him.

"I must inform you that I do not scare like other men, especially in the so-called realm of the supernatural. I wager you are merely one of the men from the tavern. Think you can have a good laugh at my expense? Your friends are probably watching from nearby. There will be no entertainment for you tonight. I am on to your trickster ways. Be off with you, man. Go try to scare some little, hapless child or meek woman elsewhere. Not what you expected, now? Didn't expect to come across such a fearless man as I in the dark of night? What do you have to say to that?"

The headless rider remained still. Shaunessy watched him with genuinely no fear. He scoffed at him and turned up his nose.

"Let us go, boy. We shall leave our trickster friend here to sit alone on his horse in the cold and dark."

Shaunessy turned and began to gallop away. He smiled to himself.

"Is this the fearful Legend of Sleepy Hollow? A man in a costume. I should go back and rip it off of him, and see who the prankster is underneath."

He laughed as he turned his head again to look at the rider. His laughing ceased.

The rider was directly behind his horse. The nose of the

hellish horse, with its eyes fully glowing red, was mere inches from the rump of Shaunessy's horse. The headless rider seemed to be much taller in its saddle and towered over the now-frightened Shaunessy.

"I am not frightened of you!" Shaunessy yelled as he stopped his horse in its tracks.

The headless rider rode up alongside him.

"Who's underneath your costume?"

Shaunessy reached across to the headless rider, to touch the opening where a head should be. A disturbing cackle exploded from the opening, startling Shaunessy to the point of almost falling off his horse. Shaunessy's horse bolted in fear as Shaunessy barely pulled himself back on his saddle with one hand, grabbing the reins—his other hand was locked in an iron grip on the lantern. It took him a few moments to settle himself properly on his fleeing horse.

He told himself not to look.

Shaunessy glanced back. Though it was quarter of a mile away now, the Headless Horseman's laugh sounded louder. It held onto its hellish horse with one hand, and in the other was some kind of fiery, orange projectile. The goblin horse rose up on its hind legs and held in the air for a moment. When its forelegs touched the ground, it raced after them with a speed Shaunessy had never seen in all his years.

"Run, boy!"

Shaunessy was filled with nothing but fear as he frantically tried to get his horse to run faster.

"No!" Shaunessy yelled. "I refuse to believe in you!"

He threw himself off his horse. Shaunessy fell to the ground violently and watched his terrified horse race away down the road, as if on fire. The lantern had flown from his hand and hit the ground, smashing to pieces. All there was, all he could see, was the dark night.

But it was not dark for long.

He blindly stood to his feet, and then his eyes perceived an approaching glow. It was the Horseman racing to him. The orange glow from his pumpkin projectile brightened the area brighter than ten lanterns.

Shaunessy stood his ground as the galloping goblin horse neared him with his master at breakneck speed.

"I don't believe in you! Therefore, you cannot hurt me!"

The Horseman threw its pumpkin.

It hit Finn Shaunessy with a force that picked him off the cold ground and carried him through the air. He felt a flash of unimaginable pain and screamed with a maniacal intensity; then no sound at all came from his lungs. Unnatural flames enveloped his body that changed from orange to red to white. He watched his body, from his shoulders down, disintegrate to ashes until all that remained was his head.

Shaunessy's horse crossed the threshold into the town of Sleepy Hollow, running blind and driven only by fear. It could see the approaching light behind it. It could feel the growing fire. The horse could now see the bridge it approached.

Shaunessy's fiery head hit the horse's side with tremendous force, knocking it into the river. The horse disappeared into the water's depths. Shaunessy's head rolled along the ground to the river. A blur raced by as the Headless Horseman dipped down from his goblin horse, grabbed the head, and was gone.

Part II
The Gang

Baltimore

"I knew of them long before they knew of me, long before they set out to trespass into my domain. There were ten of them. He was the first man."

The black bird landed on the tallest point in town, which was the pinnacle of the triangular roof of the church tower. It had followed the man for many days and many miles for its master.

The disturbing image was the first thing that caught his eye when he first entered the building. An old portrait hung off to one side of the wall, among an assortment of both small and large nature paintings—each one masterfully done, and should have drawn his attention instead. But for some reason, it was the old portrait that he was drawn to. It was of an old man standing tall in a fine suit; clearly he was important if his likeness adorned the building's wall, or was supposed to be. But the artist's intent to be as realistic as possible resulted in a grotesque likeliness of the man. The elderly man's head had no hair, and his face was so gaunt that his head was nothing more than a human skull with a covering of skin. The worst of it was the eyes—the pupils were too big and seemed more like empty holes drilled into the bone.

Why would they have such an unsettling painting, let alone display it in public? he thought. *Was the artist trying, in a clever way, to say something malevolent about the man?*

For an instant, he felt a twinge within his gut to stop everything, walk out of the place, and never come back. It felt like it was that kind of a moment. But, of course, he didn't.

"Baltimore," he answered.

"You're from the city of Baltimore?" the man in the brown bowler hat asked him.

"No. My name's Baltimore. Chief Baltimore."

"Chief? That's a funny name for an Indian. Never heard of an Indian named after a city. Were you born there?"

"No. Born out West. Ohio Territory."

"Chief of what tribe?"

"The tribe no longer exists. So I had no objections when I appointed myself chief," he said jokingly.

"An Indian chief with no tribe. How long have you been a tracker?"

"All my life."

"I also never seen an Indian dressed like you. An expensive, and inappropriate, outfit for a tracker."

"I like to wear fine things."

Baltimore had shoulder length hair under his cowboy hat. His face was clean-shaven, and his skin was a dark tan. With the exception of his hat, his dark clothes were that of a wealthy upper-class gentleman.

"What about out in the wild, on the trail, after a dangerous fugitive? Those clothes won't be much use to you."

"I manage."

"Why are you here?"

"I'm here for the job."

"I don't think you're what we want."

The man in the bowler hat stood at a table. On either side of him sat a few men each. It was Baltimore's turn, and he had been waiting outside the bank for his interview for nearly an hour before they called him in. The robbery happened earlier in the morning, and the news spread faster than the thieves had escaped the area. Baltimore considered himself fortunate to be in the right place at the right time and didn't have any qualms about the wait.

"How have the other men that you hired performed?" Baltimore asked.

The bowler man looked at him but did not answer. He then looked at his colleagues seated at the table.

Baltimore continued, "You don't have your money and you don't have the bank thieves."

"No, we don't. But I don't think any Indian in fancy dress will find them any better than the ones we've already hired."

"How much are you paying?"

"You? Nothing. Because we ain't hiring you."

Baltimore had an unconcerned expression on his face. "That's even better then."

"Better? Better how?"

"I'm going after the money, regardless, and if I don't have an agreement with you, I'll kill the bank thieves and keep the whole booty for myself."

"Hold on there." One of the men—probably the bank

owner—stood from the table. "The bank can work something out with you as easily as we did with the rest of the men we hired."

"How good are ya?" asked another man.

"I'm the best tracker you'll ever meet in your entire life."

"Not very modest, are you?" the main man said.

"Tell us about yourself first," the man in the bowler hat demanded. "What was this Indian tribe you say you were in?"

"It was a great tribe," Baltimore answered.

"What happened?"

"*You* happened. Whites came in, and new diseases came with them. Almost every man, woman, and child died from plague." The men were now uncomfortable. Baltimore held up his hand. "Oh, I'm not blaming anyone. It happened to my father's ancestors in Europe when the plague did the same to you."

"Indians in Europe?" the bowler man asked.

"My father was a White man." Baltimore smiled. "I come from a long line of warriors on both my father's side—going all the way back to the Vikings—and my mother's side—through the Patuxet tribe of the Wampanoag Confederation."

"Vikings?"

"Your father took an Indian wife?" another man asked.

"My father was one of the earliest settlers to this land. He lived with the Wampanoag people."

"Oh, he went Indian," bowler man said.

Baltimore laughed. "Not as rare as people would like to admit."

"And now you're going White," bowler man said.

Baltimore chuckled again. "I've gone 'city.' Not the same thing. Just living both sides of my family tree. I'll always be Indian, as you say."

"Well, Mister, if you can track these men, what compensation do you want?" the main man asked.

"I take one percent of the total."

All the men were taken aback.

"If I bring it back, you count it, and you hand over one percent."

"That's a lot of money, mister," the bowler man said. "We're not paying any of them that. We're giving you the same flat fee reward as the other men."

"That won't do. One percent. That's my fee. You see that I like to wear fine things. Do we have a deal?"

"If we don't have to pay for any expense money up-front, then yes," the main man answered reluctantly.

"One addition, though," the bowler man interjected. "I go along, and so do a couple of my men."

"Why didn't you accompany the other men you hired?"

"Because they didn't pretend to be a great tracker. I want to see how a supposed great tracker works in real life."

Baltimore said, "I have no objections. I was about to ask what you wanted done with the bank thieves, but you've already answered the question. I'll track the money and you'll capture or kill the thieves. Is that the plan?"

"That's the plan."

Baltimore spoke to every person who had witnessed the robbery, both inside the bank and outside. There were six gunmen, and the only person to get killed was a Good Samaritan who foolishly tried to stop the thieves and got a bullet in the chest for his trouble. The bank thieves struck when there wasn't a lawman anywhere within close distance.

Everyone noticed that the Indian spent an excessive amount of time asking about the thieves—how they looked, clothes, how they walked, their disposition, their voices, if anyone talked, what they said, who seemed to be the leader. The thieves were well-disciplined in the execution of the robbery and, besides saying to one of the employees, "Give us every bit of money in the bank or we'll kill you all and take it anyway," they spoke no other words, but menacingly waved their guns in everyone's face.

Baltimore then spent even more time asking about the bank thieves' horses—every detail from color, height, distinguishing marks, color and condition of the saddles, any saddlebags, etc. It seemed that his questions would never end, and the man in the bowler hat had grown more impatient and flustered with every passing minute.

The bank manager was of a different opinion. "He's being thorough. Professionals are thorough." The man in the bowler hat buried his impatience.

The Indian went outside the bank and crouched down low to the ground to study the dirt. Sometimes he would stare at an area quietly for a while, and then he'd stand up for a wider view.

"I don't think you'll be able to pull any tracks out of this. Everyone has been through here dozens of times already," the man with the bowler said.

Baltimore ignored him and spent another hour in front of the bank, circling around it, moving up and down the street, and then followed in the direction he was told the bank thieves made their getaway on horseback. He was almost three miles away when he stopped and casually walked back to the back where the bank's men were impatiently waiting—not just the man in the bowler hat anymore—chewing tobacco, smoking pipes, or drinking coffee.

"For a tracker, you sure spend a lot of time not tracking anything," the man with the bowler hat snapped.

"We can leave now. I know where they went," Baltimore said as he walked by.

"What?" said one of the men. "You know where they are? How? We have about a dozen men out after them and they all came back saying they lost them."

Baltimore smiled as he glanced back at them, but did not stop as he headed to the livery stables.

A few moments into their ride, from the chatter of the men, Baltimore learned the man in the bowler hat was named Stern. Baltimore didn't care about the names of the other three men; they were the hired thugs. Stern was a lifelong employee of the bank. He probably wasn't a good employee, but he made up for that in loyalty. Whatever the bank needed to be done, he'd be there. Half the day was already gone but they rode out of Boston anyway, at Baltimore's insistence.

"I still don't believe you can find them," Stern said to him.

"I can find anything that moves along the earth," Baltimore said back without looking at him.

"They're probably down in Virginia by now."

"They're not all that far away."

"How can you possibly know that? You can't tell all that by reading dirt on the ground."

"Reading tracks is but one small part of tracking your prey. There are more important things than that."

"Pray? What does praying to the Almighty have to do with this?"

"Prey. As in the fox hunts its prey."

"Oh, prey."

"Tracking is also knowing all about your prey, their habits and abilities, and anticipating what they're likely to do. It's also knowing all about your own strengths and weaknesses so when those times come, and they will, that the prey does the unexpected, you can still be successful."

"Tracking is all that, huh? It's good that you're the tracker because I don't have any patience for all that."

Baltimore looked at Stern and smiled. He glanced at the pistol on Stern's belt. "Have you ever used that?"

"Why do you ask?"

"Your men here, I know they have shot plenty of men. But aren't you simply a bank employee who sits in a chair in an office and counts money? Do you know how to use that gun?"

Stern's face turned red with anger. "I know how to use a gun. I had to during the War."

"The War was thirteen years ago. Have you picked it up since?"

"No, but if I have to shoot one of those bank robbers, then I will do what I need to do."

"Make sure you do because the group is only as strong as its weakest man."

Stern got madder. "Where's your pistol? You have a nerve carrying no gun yourself. Indian, don't concern yourself with me. Track the men, keep your mouth closed, and we'll do what we need to do when we find them. If we find them. I still don't believe you're this great tracker that you claim to be with those fancy clothes of yours."

Baltimore smiled and said nothing else. The other three men remained quiet as they watched with amusement.

The more they rode, the fewer the signs of any kind of human presence. Stern nervously looked around at the countryside that soon became forest. They followed the Indian riding his beautiful, brown Mustang at a steady pace. The men noticed that he never looked out to see where he was going, but kept his gaze down at the ground, scanning side-to-side, and, at the most, several feet ahead.

"Where are you taking us?" Stern finally asked. "They wouldn't have come out this way. There's nothing out here. You must be lost."

Baltimore ignored him and kept moving.

Stern was flustered again. He looked around and now noticed that the ground was getting rockier as they approached a river. In the distance, they could see the cliffs of the nearing mountains. The land was beautiful, but not to Stern.

"You're lost. I can tell. You're trying to pretend like you know what you're doing, where you're going, but you're lost as a blind idiot."

A smiling Baltimore stopped his horse when it was about to enter a shallow patch of the river. The men watched him as he scanned the ground and then followed some kind of invisible path with his eyes. He looked up to the cliffs.

"What are you doing?" Stern asked.

"Tracking."

Stern huffed in frustration again. "Tracking what?"

Baltimore glanced at him again for a moment, then turned to the other three men and declared, "They're up there."

All four men perked up and looked up at the cliff in unison.

"What? Where?" Stern asked.

Baltimore ignored him and spoke to the three men. "I'd ride through," he said pointing, "with the trees and brush as cover and come at them from their flank. Be quiet though, in case one of them is watching. They might even be sleeping, thinking no one could possibly follow them here."

The three men looked at Stern for instructions, but saw the indecision on his face. One of them laughed, and the three men set out on their horses.

"Wait for me," Stern said to them, but the three men ignored him.

"You might not want to call out again," Baltimore said. "Makes it difficult to sneak up on bank thieves."

Stern gave him a disgusted look and rode forward, then stopped.

"What are you going to do?"

Stern was determined *not* to keep his voice down.

"I'm waiting here for you and your men to capture the bad guys. You said yourself, I carry no gun. I did my job already, now it's your turn."

Stern huffed again and rode off.

Baltimore watched him disappear into the trees after his men. He sat and took in the sight of the beautiful terrain with the clear water of the rushing river. The fool Stern had no sense of stealth. Hopefully, the sounds of rushing water was enough to muffle his loud mouth.

Baltimore's horse moved a bit into the river to take a drink.

He expected everything to go smoothly. The three men would surprise the six bank thieves. They probably were told by Stern, or the bank manager, to shoot them on sight. Maybe the bank thieves would be lucky, and they would be bound up and set upon their own horses. Then they would all ride back, and he'd collect his percentage and be off on his way to the next job.

Bam! The shot jolted Baltimore from his thoughts.

Both he and his horse looked in the direction of the sound. They heard a man scream and then an explosion of gunfire.

Stern's three hired guns cowered behind a boulder as the bank robbers fired off another few shots.

"Did Stern fall or did they get him?" one of them asked.

"They got him. He fell down the mountain," another answered.

"Don't feel so bad about it," said the other. "If they hadn't shot him, then it would have been one of us."

One of the men began to peer over the rock when a shot rang out and hit the boulder right near his eye, showering him with rock fragments and dust. He yelled out, startled, as he grabbed part of his face and ducked down.

The man who fired the shot was the only bank robber nearby—positioned ten yards away from the bounty hunters. He had already reloaded and aimed to fire at the three men again with a smile on his face. Never did he come across such a dumb set of men. *But how did they track us?*

His five fellow bank robbers slowly circled the bounty

hunters' location from the other side of the plateau, with guns in hand. Their lead man peeked above the ridge. They were directly behind the hunters—one of the bounty hunters was holding the left side of his face above the eye, wincing in pain, and the other two men were crouched behind the boulder with their backs to them.

He slowly aimed his gun as he glanced back at his gang, smiling. He nodded to gesture them to do the same. They all tried to stifle any laughter.

The lead man was about to give the final signal. *An arrow hit him in the shoulder.*

He yelled out as he dropped to the ground. The other four men turned to fire when a second arrow hit another man in the lower leg, collapsing him to the ground. The remaining three men scrambled.

The two uninjured bounty hunters appeared behind the bank robbers, with guns aimed.

"Stop where you are!" one of them yelled.

The three robbers stopped and fired at them as the two bounty hunters returned fire. An explosion of five guns, nearly simultaneously, but no one was hit. One of the bank robbers threw his gun at one of the hunters and then rushed at him. An arrow hit him in the lower leg and he yelled out. The two bounty hunters cowered, not knowing if they should run or stay still.

The remaining bank robbers dove to the ground. One of them pulled another gun from his jacket. The two bounty hunters turned and ran. The armed robber rose from the ground as an arrow struck his gun hand, and his weapon fell to the ground.

"Who's shooting arrows at us?" the bank robber yelled.

The two bounty hunters returned with fresh rifles,

aiming at him.

"Will you surrender now, or do we have to kill you?" one of them asked.

The robber glared back at them and pretended not to see his final comrade in the distance, coming around behind the two bounty hunters to strike.

An arrow rose through the air, over them, and disappeared. Two bounty hunters craned their necks before hearing a man's voice yell out and more gunfire.

"Help me," Stern begged.

Stern was lying on his back on the ground, holding his bloody gut with both hands, with dust and dirt all over his clothes. He stared at an approaching Baltimore, with a bow in one hand and a few long, thin black arrows in the other. Baltimore stopped. Stern's eyes were wide with fear and he was crying.

"I don't want to die like this," he said to Baltimore.

"I'll get help from your men."

"No, don't leave me here."

"You will die, but not today," Baltimore said looking away from the chest wound as he moved past. "I'll get your men, and I'll patch you up. Promise."

Stern just watched him from the ground, crying.

Baltimore climbed up to the plateau of the mountain where the bounty hunters had dragged all the injured bank robbers together.

"We didn't see you had a bow and arrows," one of the bounty hunters said.

"I keep it in my magic pouch," Baltimore said. "All Indians have one."

He studied the bank robbers.

"If it weren't for you, Indian, this hapless bunch would have been dead, and we'd be on our way to Mexico," the smiling leader of the robbers said.

"Did you enjoy the show?" Baltimore asked.

"Yes, indeed. Especially the arrow shot to the gunhand. That was a great shot. I don't know any man who could have made that shot. And look at how you're dressed. To be taken down—hardened no-good thieves such as ourselves—by a man dressed in fancy attire like you. Embarrassing."

Baltimore smiled.

"It was you, wasn't it? You were the one who tracked us. Not this hapless bunch."

"That's enough from you," said one of the bounty hunters, pointing his rifle.

"I'm glad I could entertain." Baltimore said and then motioned to the bounty hunters. "I trust you can handle this alone. I'll go back down and patch up Stern."

The men nodded.

Baltimore leaned down to Stern to examine the chest wound. To Stern, the amount of blood was an indication that he'd soon be at death's door. Baltimore knew, when he first glanced at it, that the *lack* of blood meant it was only a minor wound.

"You are a lucky man," Baltimore said. "If we were back at my tribe, we would have called you 'Man With the Chest of Iron.' Bullets don't go through you, they bounce off you."

"How do you mean?"

"The bullet bounced off this key on the necklace under

your shirt."

"It's a tiny key."

"If anyone asks, I'll say it bounced off your bare chest. Some people have a hard head. You have a hard gut."

Baltimore smiled at him and Stern finally managed one himself.

"I thought I was going to die."

"I told you, one day, but not today. Not for a long time."

"You warned me. They probably heard my big mouth, and I walked right into an ambush."

"Why worry about it? The bank thieves are caught. Your men are alive. You're alive. All you need is rest. No harm done. We'll get you on your horse and, this time next week, you'll be filling your iron belly with all the ale you can put your hands on."

"Yes, I will do that."

Baltimore took off his fancy jacket and then took off his shirt to rip it into three long strips. He then tightly wrapped up Stern's chest and tied the ends. He pulled on them to ensure they were secure. Baltimore stood up as he put his jacket back on and helped Stern get to his feet. Stern winced from pain but, once standing, was fine.

"We'll keep your chest bound up until we get you back to town."

"But you ripped up your fine shirt for me."

"No need to fret. I'll soon have new money and then I can buy a lot more fine shirts. You'll have your ale. I'll have my clothes."

Stern hadn't actually stared death in the face, but he felt he had. "I'm never going to be an irritable idiot ever again."

"That is how to live one's life. Find the good, even in the bad in life. Here." Baltimore reached out and put something into Stern's hand, and then closed it. "The bullet. Hang it around your neck. The bullet that was no match for you."

"I hope one day I'll get to repay the favor, Mr. Baltimore."

Baltimore smiled. "No need. Helping someone in need is sufficient payment for me. You wait here, and I'll bring down your horse." He turned his head to look at the mountain path. "I'll only be..."

Baltimore glanced back to see an angry grimace on Stern's face. There was no time to react as Stern violently pushed him back with all his strength. The Chief crashed backwards to the ground. *A six-foot long, black spear sliced into the ground at the very spot he stood!* A shocked Baltimore jumped to his feet and both men stared up into the sky.

In all his years, he had seen them pick up many kinds of objects, and even animals that seemed impossible for them to carry, but never such a weapon. Baltimore felt in his gut that it was he, not Stern or any of the other men here on the plateau that had escaped a horrible death. His throat tightened, imagining it in his mind—impaled through his head and down through his body to the ground.

The black bird flew away. It had to return to its master and answer for its failure.

The Austrian

"There were ten of them. He was the second man."

Two men trotted their horses as fast as possible through the bustling New York streets. They looked like twins, dressed nearly all in black—hat, clothes, and boots—with bushy mustaches and hurried looked on their faces. A carriage followed right behind them, and the driver pulled to a stop on the harbor street.

"How will we know him?" one horseman asked.

"They said we'd know him when we see him," answered the carriage driver.

From the break of dawn to sundown, the seaport was nothing short of a madhouse. Laborers unloaded and loaded goods. An array of boats and ships—both tiny and enormous—were always arriving and departing. Seaman arrived, and others boarded. Merchants and other town onlookers comprised the crowds.

Passengers disembarked from one of the transatlantic ships. The two men joined the crowds of people—families waiting for loved ones, employers waiting for new employees, and businessmen waiting for colleagues.

The men watched every arriving passenger. Nearly half an hour passed before all the passengers were off the ship and the crowd dispersed, only the two men and carriage driver remained. Then they saw him—the last passenger. The Austrian was a finely dressed man—a narrow hat, thin build, and stringy mustache. He carried two pieces of luggage with him; a medium suitcase in his left hand and a long, slender case in his right. He saw the two men and walked directly to them.

"Gentlemen," he said to them.

"Do we have the pleasure of meeting the Austrian?"

"You do. May we go directly to your boss?"

"Don't you want to at least eat first and settle in? They reserved a good room for you at the local inn."

"That's not necessary. I'm eager to begin."

"Shall we carry your bags?"

"Thank you." He handed them the one suitcase. "I will keep this one with me," he said, referring to the slender case.

The man opened the door of the waiting carriage.

"All this luxury and expense on my account?" the Austrian asked as he climbed into the carriage, and the man closed the door.

"Mr. Tasker likes to start all his business relations in the most positive way."

The carriage moved slowly through the busy streets with the two riders following behind. They arrived at the center of the business district and slowed to a stop in front of a series of office buildings.

They led the Austrian into the largest of the buildings and upstairs to one of the rooms. Two men waited—a younger man in a dark suit with intense eyes; and an older, distinguished man in a lighter suit with graying brown hair, mustache, and a full beard.

The Victorian-styled room reminded the Austrian more of a royal sitting room than a common office.

"Johannes," the younger man said to the Austrian as he approached to shake his hand.

"Richard," the Austrian said to him. "Good to see my comrade in arms after all these many years."

The younger man smiled as he asked, "How was your trip?"

"Long, too long, and uneventful, but I managed."

"I cannot admit to ever wanting to be confined to a floating box on the high seas ever again, which is what I feel all ships are, to be honest, no matter how advanced they become."

"Ah, but Richard, there is an entire world out there for you to see."

Richard laughed a bit. "There is an entire world right here on solid ground in America for me. And beyond our Atlantic coast cities and towns, the entirety of the West is untamed, unexplored territory, but we can ponder about that perhaps at dinner." He turned to the older man next to him. "This is my father."

The Austrian shook the man's hand. "Mr. Tasker."

"My son has spoken of you often. I was intrigued when he spoke of an overseas comrade known as The Austrian."

"I have spoken often of your son in my own country."

"Please, let's get comfortable."

The older Tasker led them to a round table in the room, and the men took their seats.

"I don't know much about your home country of Austria. I should know more with all our growing overseas business interests, but my son handles that."

"It's between German and Italy," the younger Tasker said to his father.

"How long was your sea journey?" Mr. Tasker asked.

"Approximately six weeks," the Austrian answered.

"Such voyages can be unpleasant and dangerous, even for the wealthy. You did not come all this way only at my son's request."

"I would have, but no, I have other business in America and intend to remain here for at least a few years."

"How do you like your hotel accommodations?"

"I haven't seen them yet, but I have no doubt they are splendid."

"They didn't take you to your accommodations?" Mr. Tasker looked annoyed.

"It was not their fault. It was my decision. I wanted to be brought here immediately."

"After such a long time on the ship, I would have thought you'd want to relax, freshen up, and even take a nap now that you're firmly planted on solid earth," the younger Tasker said.

"I made sure to get double the sleep the day before. I'm eager to start, if I can, indeed, help."

Richard Tasker clasped his hands together on the table as he began. "I tried to be as detailed in my letter as I could, but I'm sure you have many questions."

"Why don't you begin with telling me exactly what the problem is and why you think I am the only one who can help you?"

"The latter part is obvious."

"The invention is supposed to be confidential. No one must know of it."

"But when the public does know of it, it won't be long until everyone has one."

"That may be true, in fact, I have no doubt of it, but its existence must remain unknown, nonetheless."

The elder Tasker looked at both men. "Invention?"

"I haven't even told my father. But that can be discussed later. I am sure you recollect my frequent accounts of my childhood sweetheart."

"Yes. The fine young woman you were to be married to. Indeed, I expected that would have come to pass and you would be the proud father of your own brood already."

Richard Tasker smiled for a moment, but then it disappeared from his face to be replaced by distress.

"The problem is that she is being held hostage, as are her parents and an entire town. I'm sure one of your questions is why we haven't engaged local law officials. The fact of the matter is that these renegades are the official law."

"Who are these men?"

"Mr. Brunner," the elder Tasker began, "during the War, the British hired tens of thousands of Hessian soldiers to fight against our Continental Army. I was told that they made up nearly a quarter of the British forces. They were vicious cut-throats worthy of their dubious reputation."

"The British hired the Germans to fight you. Americans enlisted the French to fight the British," the Austrian said. "Both sides hired Indians, too. Personally, I prefer the Germans over the French."

"Why is that?" the elder Tasker asked.

"Do you know what's happening in France with their

Revolution?"

The elder Tasker nodded. "We've heard."

"The sheer scope of the human butchery happening on their French streets is unimaginable. The excuse is to overthrow its monarchy too, but the monarchy is gone, and the killing has not stopped. I cannot imagine the Germans ever participating in that kind of slaughter of innocents, ever."

The elder Tasker said, "All wars have their own unique atrocities."

"Indeed. Sorry," he said to him. "Please continue."

Richard began again. "These Hessians control the town and they are vicious animals. The people are literally prisoners."

"Do you know about the story of the Headless Horseman?" the elder Tasker asked, playfully.

"Headless Horseman?" The Austrian was intrigued. "I have never heard of such a thing."

"It's a well-known ghost story in these parts."

"Never mind that, Father. We can acquaint him with local ghost stories another time."

"If he's going to be living here, then he should know of it," the elder Tasker added. He looked back to the Austrian. "The Horseman in the ghost story was also supposed to be a Hessian too. Had his head blown completely off in the War, and then was condemned to ride in the dead of night in search of his head. The point of me bringing it up is that these Hessians are using the story to hold the town."

"How?"

"They have the people believing that they, too, cannot be killed," Mr. Tasker answered.

The Austrian tried to contain his amusement. "Cannot be killed?"

"Even the Indians are scared of this town, and no White lawman nearby will intervene to help us," Richard said.

"And you naturally thought of me and the invention."

"Yes. Not only can you kill them, you can kill all of them in the blink of an eye."

The Austrian thought for a moment. "I'm going to ask you a question—"

"Ask us anything. My father and I have nothing to hide. This is a dangerous endeavor."

"The question I'm going to ask is of a delicate nature. You must know, I am asking to gather information and not to upset or embarrass you in any way. Do you understand?"

Richard's face got somber. "I understand."

"What is the occupation of your lady in question?"

Richard's face turned red. "Why does that matter? She's being held against her will. The entire town is being held against their will by these German Hessian animals. They should never have been allowed to come here."

"I was informed that most of them returned to Germany after the War."

"Not all of them."

"The ones who remained settled into the country like every other nationality. There are British here, too," the elder Tasker added.

"They should never have been allowed to stay here either."

Tasker Sr. glanced at his now angry son, but continued. "Our quarrel is not with former pro-British German soldiers, pro-British British, or any Tories who reside in

America. The War, thank God, is over."

"Your woman is a hostage?"

"She is."

"This is not a personal grudge against Hessians, which I know personally killed relatives of your family during the War?"

"No, our quarrel is with these Germans."

"I do not care either way, but we have to be honest with ourselves. I've seen too many men killed because they were too proud to acknowledge their own flaws. I am far from perfect, but I know what my flaws are so that I can recognize bad behavior in myself that could get me killed. All men must know their own selves. Again, I don't care either way. Do you understand?"

"Yes, we do," the elder Tasker answered.

"The matter that troubles me is this story you told me about the reputation of these men. Superstition can be quite powerful with people. I have seen so in my own home country and nearby. Men can be dangerous enough on their own, but if they start to believe their own fantasy, such as they are supernatural beings unable to be killed like other natural men, then the situation becomes much more dangerous."

"I can see that my son was wise to seek you out," the elder man said. "You are looking at this whole situation with a fresh perspective."

"I want to make it clear that she does want to be rescued," Richard interjected. "You needn't have any doubts about that. I admit—I know that's in your mind from a previous letter of mine."

"More than one," the Austrian added.

"Yes, before this all happened, yes, we parted bitterly.

But we reconciled and we're more together than we've ever been. Then this happened. I would not risk our lives otherwise. Nor would my father support me in this endeavor otherwise. It is exactly as we characterize."

"Will you help my son, Mr. Brunner?" the man asked.

The Austrian was quiet for a moment. "Richard, what do you propose to be our plan of attack?"

"I'll ride into town with my father's rifle and rescue her. You remain outside and kill any of these Hessians that come after us."

"It sounds so simple and straightforward when you say it."

"I know it won't be, but that's my plan of attack."

The Austrian nodded. "Good. Then, I will help you."

The elder Tasker smiled. "Excellent!"

"Then we'll be even," Richard said.

The Austrian shook his head. "No, I will still owe you. You saved my life. I am only helping you in a matter of need."

"No, Johannes. She is my life. You will be saving my life too."

The Austrian looked at the father. "Richard was always the romantic. Young people in love. What can you do?"

The elder Tasker laughed. "Yes, what can you do?"

The Austrian and Richard rode out at first light.

"Isn't it better to go in at night," Richard had asked.

"It would, but I cannot see in the dark," the Austrian answered.

It was daytime but the sky was overcast and, as they neared the town, they could see it was surrounded by fog.

"Is this going to be a problem?" Richard asked him.

"No, but I'm going to have to be closer to the town than

I would like. You concentrate on your lady. I will concern myself with the logistics of my own attack."

"Two things I am certain of. I will rescue my Alice and these Hessians will soon pay for their barbarity."

The Austrian's friend was always cocky in whatever he did, and there was no point in trying to change him.

They decided on the point of entry. Richard disappeared on foot into the fog. The Austrian had also dismounted and secured the reins of his horse to the same tree. While Richard skulked into town with his father's rifle in hand, the Austrian watched the town, holding his long, slender wooden case by the handle. He thought to himself that the whole situation would make a great ghost story—darkened skies during the day with thick fog circling a town run by supernatural Hessian ex-soldiers.

Richard crouched down on the roof of one of the two-story buildings in town with his rifle firmly clutched in his hands. He listened to the voices and activity of the rooms right beneath him and outside the window from the ground below. It seemed the fog made the people want to limit their outside activity and remain indoors. Some of the voices he heard were English, but occasionally he'd hear loud talking in another foreign language.

He looked down and finally saw that no one was around. He crawled down the side of the roof and pushed opened a window to an empty room before he threw his rifle inside, and then quickly jumped in.

Thirty minutes later, his head popped up to peer out from one of the ground-level windows. He disappeared again, and then the nearby door began to open. Richard slowly exited, holding his rifle in one hand and in his other, the hand of a woman. She was a petite woman with fair skin and blonde hair, wearing a bright blue dress. He gave her a reassuring look.

"We're almost free," he said and she nodded.

They both ran out of the building together into the fog that was enveloping the town streets. They both stopped in their tracks. Shadowy figures came out of the fog.

Richard pointed his rifle. "I swear, I will shoot you dead!"

His lady stood closely behind him with a look of fear on her face. He had his sights targeted on the largest of the men slowly walking to them out of the fog. He was the most fearful of the lot. The men laughed and joked as they drew nearer, and Richard and his lady backed away.

"This was not a wise plan," one of the thugs said in a foreign accent. "You only have one rifle. You are one man. We are many."

Several men stood before Richard and the woman, but then they could see the figures of a dozen more men coming out from the fog. All of the men moved closer with smiles and smirks on their faces, none making any provocative moves, but all were armed with pistols.

"After you shoot one of us," the same German man said, "what do you suppose will happen then? Do you think you will live? Do you think your woman will escape punishment? We will punish her, you know." He looked at the woman. "Did you tell your man how we often punish you?"

"Shut up!" she yelled at them.

"You are pointing your rifle at the law of this town," the large man said to Richard. His voice was deep and as menacing as his gaze; his accent made it even more so.

"The punishment for trying to kill a lawman is death. "

"You are no lawmen," the woman yelled. "You are criminals!"

The men continued to surround the two of them. Richard looked around into fog. The fear in his face was obvious. He leaned his head back to her and whispered, "When I tell you to run, you run."

"No, I can't do that," she whispered back.

"You have to listen to me. It will be all right. I didn't come alone. Run out of town and I'll be right behind you."

"They'll kill you."

"I have no intentions of being killed in this town. Get ready to run."

"Are you planning to run?" one of the German men called out. "That will be a mistake. The woman may get a little distance away, but we will shoot you dead. Then we'll chase her down and punish her."

"I will kill you personally," the large man said to Richard.

"Run!" Richard yelled as he fired.

The shot was aimed at the large man and hit him squarely in the face. The giant man fell back to the ground.

The other men all drew their pistols in unison, and Richard looked back to see that she listened to him. She ran into the fog. He turned his head back to them and waited for his end.

He heard a strange sound whiz through the air and one of the men yelled out. The man grabbed his neck as he fell. One after another, men cried out and fell as they were shot in rapid fashion, one second after the next. In less than a minute, all the men were on the ground, dead or dying.

Richard exhaled a sigh of relief. A figure ran through

the fog—it was her. He dropped his rifle and ran to her. They embraced each other. Richard looked up and saw another figure approaching him—it was the Austrian carrying his unique rifle in his right hand. To Richard, it was still the most beautiful weapon he had ever seen.

"I see you have found your fine lady," he said.

"Yes, I did," Richard said. "I see the fog was no hindrance for you."

The Austrian looked at the bodies strewn out on the ground. "Neither were they."

"Alice," Richard said. "This is my good friend, Johannes."

The Austrian was about to greet her when they heard another voice.

"Johannes," echoed from the mouth of one of the Hessian bodies on the ground.

They all looked and saw the body of the largest man sit up from the ground. His face was blown off, and what looked at them was a head that was half-face, half-skull.

"Johannes, the Austrian," the dead man said as it rose to its feet.

The Austrian, Richard, and Alice stood there frozen in shock; unable to move, unable to comprehend what they were seeing.

The dead man was on its feet and lurched towards the Austrian. "Johannes," it said again as it drew its pistol and aimed at the Austrian's head. "Johannes, the Austrian, will not hurt my master."

The Austrian stood and watched helplessly. Then its zombie head exploded. The dead man collapsed to the ground.

A small, grizzled man with a rifle ran to the scene with

a mean look on his face.

"I shot you good! I swore I'd get ya! I told you I would! I'd punish you! I told you if anyone ever kilt all your men, that I would be there to make sure I kilt you for what you did! I told ya!"

The small man leaned down to the large dead man, and his face turned pale white. He dropped his rifle as he grabbed his mouth and ran off. He only made it a few paces before vomiting.

The three of them looked back at the large dead man—the dead man who was dead again, or was he?

"Master?" Richard asked. "Who is that? What did he mean? How did he know your name? He never met … He never saw you before. But he was going to kill you. But you killed him."

The Austrian wasn't listening. He stood and stared with a vacant, wide-eyed look on his face, his mouth slightly open, paralyzed in shock.

Wrangler

"There were ten of them. He was the third man."

They spotted the man from miles away, across the vast open plain—a lone dot walking to them, no horse in sight. As he came closer, the six-man team of cattle herders made out each new feature about him. He was tall and lean, wearing a brown rawhide coat with a fur collar and a brown flat-top hat. The man had very tan skin, a full black mustache, and the makings of a beard with all the stubble on his face. Over his head, and hanging around his back, was a bundle of rope. He wore a pair of sturdy pants and a worn pair of dark-brown, leather boots.

The stranger touched the tip of his hat to greet the three men at the front of the herd of prime cattle— more than a hundred in all. The riders slowed to a stop.

"Not a good place to be without a horse, mister," the lead man said to him.

"I have a horse, sir," the man answered in a thick Spanish accent. "I hid her so if, by chance, I came across unfriendly men, she'd be safe."

The lead man smirked. "How do you know we aren't?"

"I can tell. You were watching me and I was watching you."

"What would you have done if we were unfriendly men? Your horse would have been safe, but you'd be in a bad way."

"I do not think so. I am good at fighting unfriendly men."

"What's your name?"

"Quetzalcoatl Jacinto Ramirez Mendoza … "

The three riders looked at one another.

"But … everyone calls me Wrangler."

"With a name like that, I see why," one man said.

"Mr. Wrangler, know how to use the rope around your neck?" the lead man asked.

"I do. That's why men hire me. Can you use an extra man?"

A second man butted in and said, "We don't need a seventh man."

"It's good. You can pay me in food and company to the next town. I'll earn my keep by getting any strays back to the main herd."

The lead man nodded. "That sounds fair."

"Good. I'll get my horse. You don't have to wait for me."

Wrangler touched the tip of his hat again and turned to walk back in the direction he came. The three men watched him for awhile before the lead man raised his hand in the air to gesture all the men to move forward.

"He said not to wait for him," the lead man said.

Wrangler joined them three-quarters of an hour later, riding up on a dark-brown mustang to the lead man.

"I'll start work," Wrangler said to him.

"That's fine."

Wrangler turned his horse around and rode to join the three men at the back of the herd. They could see him introducing himself. He rode with them a while before breaking away to watch the herd.

They were about fifty miles south of America's Southwest Territory. The men talked about the many days their journey would take, how they missed home-cooked meals, and, especially, what they would buy with their money from the job. Wrangler learned that Mr. Clement was the lead man. Wrangler listened to them attentively, but didn't participate in the conversation himself.

The men got to see Wrangler in action a few times. Two cattle from the left flank broke off from the herd and, before the rider on that side even noticed them go, Wrangler had ridden up and directed them back to the herd with his horse. The next time, something startled several cattle near the rear and one bolted away. It hadn't gone far when Wrangler had the animal lassoed around the neck and stopped. With the rope securely wrapped around the horn of his saddle, he then lead it back to the herd before jumping down from his horse to push it along. Another time, he only needed to rush his horse to block the path of a single stray and lead it back.

"Where are you from?" one of the men asked.

It was nighttime, and the men had set up camp. Wrangler and three of the men were relaxing in front of a roaring flame and drinking coffee.

"Mexico."

"Does everyone down there have names as long and unpronounceable as yours?"

The lead man appeared with the two other men to join

them at the fire.

"No sir." Wrangler laughed. "It's just custom. In my country you have two surnames after your first name and middle name. Your first surname is the first surname of your father and your second surname is the first surname of your mother."

"All I heard was the 'quetza' part at the beginning and the Mendoza part at the end. What does the 'quetza' part even mean?"

"Feathered serpent. I think my parents played a joke on me when they named me. I don't like birds. I don't like serpents. I wouldn't like a feathered serpent."

The men chuckled. "We agree with you there," one of them said.

"You did some nice work today, Mr. Wrangler. How long have you been riding and wrangling?"

"All my life. My father taught me to ride before I could walk. Or, so they tell me. I'm not so sure I believe that. But all parents like to exaggerate."

"Yes, we do," one of the men said, smiling.

"Yes, we do," Wrangler repeated.

"You have children, Mr. Wrangler?"

"Three boys."

"Where are they?"

"Back in Mexico. I used to work only there, but there is so much more work in the new United States so I work here half the year, and then go back to my wife and boys when I'm done. We can live well from what I make."

"I'm sure you do."

"You have children too, sir?"

"A boy and a girl."

"A little girl," said the second man.

"You?" Wrangler asked another man.

"He's shy," the lead man said.

"Five boys and three girls," the third man said.

"You have to watch out for the quiet ones," the lead man said.

"Well, my wife doesn't like to talk either so what else is there to do?"

The men started to laugh.

It was a chilly night, but the men continued to talk for hours. Wrangler learned that the men had come up from close to Mexico themselves, and the journey had already taken them several weeks. They did about six cattle runs a year, making enough money to support their families for an entire year. This particular trip was going to be a big payday for the men. However, to get that money, they had to cross dangerous country known for cattle rustlers and Indian raiders. Long travel, cold nights, and bad food—all to make a living for their families.

They all slept as close to the fire as possible, but every one of them slept with an ear open; listening for any strange sounds or disturbance from the horses or the cattle.

"Damn!"

Miles was always the first man up. He rose before dawn and checked on the herd. He had an uncanny ability to count the entire herd in an impossibly short amount of time. None of the men knew how he did it, but he always knew if any of the herd was missing.

"Twenty of them are gone," he said to the other men gathered around him.

"Are you positive?" the lead man asked.

"I'm positive. I'm always positive. Twenty."

"Don't concern yourselves with it," Wrangler interjected. "You do your work, and I'll find them and bring them back."

"You can't find and bring back twenty strays by yourself."

"I've done it before. You can do your work, and I'll get them back."

Wrangler went back to his sleeping place and gathered up his things. He splashed some water on his face from his canteen, mounted his horse, and rode off hard.

"You think he can get twenty cattle all by himself?" Miles asked.

"We shall see," the lead man answered.

"What's that up there?" one of the men pointed.

They could see in the distance several riders moving toward them.

"Get saddled up!" the lead man yelled.

All the men were mounted, and the lead man sat on his horse at the front with two men. Two men were situated behind them off to the side, and the last man was at the back with the herd. Each man had a pistol in his hand.

They watched them draw even closer. The strange riders were disheveled and dirty. However, that wasn't what concerned the men—these strangers looked mean and out for trouble.

The first of the strange riders was the only one with a hat, and it was pulled down low so his eyes could barely be seen. "Hello gentlemen," he said as he and his men stopped a few yards away.

"Hello," the lead man answered back.

"We see your riding a large herd in. Where you headed?"

"North. No town in particular."

"That's a lot of fine beef you got there."

The lead man said nothing.

"Here's the situation. I count six of your men, and I count eight of my men. Not a huge difference, but the odds favor us. I say you give us half the herd, and we'll be on our way without any trouble."

The strange riders all drew their pistols before he had even finished his words.

The lead man didn't answer. He kept his gaze fixed on the man doing the talking.

"If we start shooting, the herd will be scattered in every possible direction, and no one wins," he said.

"If you give us half the herd, like I said, there won't be any shooting." The leader of the cattle rustlers grinned.

"What is that?" One of the strange riders pointed past the men.

The lead man didn't dare turn his head. He kept his gaze fixed on their leader and his gun hand ready to shoot.

"They have another man coming," the rustler leader said mockingly. "You better tell your man the situation or someone will get themselves killed. He's riding in fast, and I wouldn't want him to do something without you telling him the situation..."

Something—some kind of rope weapon—flew through the air, hit the lead rustler, and, what looked like two rocks, wrapped around his neck and battered his face bloody. He fell off his horse with his eyes wide in shock and crashed headfirst to the ground.

The remaining rustlers were so shocked they froze. Wrangler rode through the men, lassoing the closest strange rider around the neck and yanking him off his horse. He rode off, dragging the man away on the ground.

"Stop him!" one of the rustlers yelled.

The cattle rustlers aimed their pistols to fire at him. The herd riders didn't hesitate; they all fired first. When the shots were over, the rustlers were dead, dying, or wounded on the ground; and their horses were running away.

They could see Wrangler jump down from his horse. He removed the rope from the rustler and got back on his horse to ride back to them. As he did, they looked at the lead rustler on the ground, his face bloody. He was dead. The rope weapon had either strangled him or pummeled him to death.

"Mr. Wrangler, I have seen many things in my life before, but I have never seen one man rescue other men from danger like that before." The lead man reached out his hand. "I'd be remiss if I didn't shake such a man's hand."

"It was nothing, sir."

"Nothing?" one of the men said. "It was definitely the opposite of nothing. What is that weapon you used?"

"How did you know they were rustlers?" the lead man asked.

"Same way I knew you weren't when we first saw each other."

"How did you know to come back?"

"I happened to look back and saw them coming, so I watched them. I knew they could be bad men. I waited, and when I was certain they were, I charged." Wrangler looked at the other man. "My weapon, you don't know it. It's called *bolas*. From my father's home country."

"Mr. Wrangler, I'm glad we happened upon you."

"And you lassoed that other man too," another said, half-laughing. "Yanked his dirty, cattle-thievin' self off his own horse."

"You can rope men as readily as cattle," said another man. "Or use that flying rope thing."

"Anything that moves, I can rope and take down, whether with my rope, or if it is further away, with my bolas."

"We believe it," Mr. Clement, the lead man, said. "We've seen it with our own eyes."

"I will leave you to do your work, and I'll get back to bringing back those strays."

"What? You don't have to do that now after what you've just done for us."

"The strays will not come back on their own, sir. I saw them in the distance before I turned back. It will not take me long to find them. I'm happy to do it."

Wrangler touched the tip of his hat and rode off hard. The men watched him for awhile and, when he disappeared over a ridge, they looked at one another.

"Well, you heard him. Let's do our work," the lead man said. "Even though they don't deserve it, give the rustlers a decent burial, and get their horses and their pistols. I saw a nice rifle on one of their horses that rode off."

Clement and his men did not set out with the herd for another hour. When they did move out, every one of the men occasionally glanced back to see if Mister Wrangler would appear.

It was nearing the end of the day, but Clement wanted to push on later than they normally would to make up for lost time, right up until the sun was setting.

As they set up camp, Miles yelled out, "Wrangler's back."

The men rushed to where Miles was standing. Wrangler rode to them with not one stray cattle, but what looked to be all of them! The steers were all roped up, one after the other, following behind him.

"Does he have all twenty of them?" one of the men asked.

"Nearly," Miles answered. "He's got nineteen."

Clement shook his head. "How did he do that?"

"We should keep him on permanently," said another one of the men.

"Yes," Clement replied. "Let's talk about it when we get to town."

A few of the men ran up to him with smiles and congratulations as Wrangler slowed to a stop. Clement walked up to him. "Amazing, Mr. Wrangler. You got them."

"Oh no, sir," he said as he dismounted from his horse. "One more is left."

"Don't worry about one steer. You did enough already."

"The one that is left is the biggest one though."

"Oh," Miles realized and turned to Clement. "The Monster."

"That one," Mr. Clement said. "We shouldn't ask Mr. Wrangler to go all the way back out there for one steer, even if it's the Monster."

"Clement, there's probably more beef on that one steer than six regular ones put together," Miles said.

"Sir, I don't mind at all. A job is not done until all of it is done. My father taught me that and it is what I teach my sons. I will get this Monster tomorrow. It will not be a problem."

The men started to laugh. "Oh, course it's not a problem. You brought back nineteen cattle all by yourself. We've never seen anyone do that, so one steer won't be anything to you," Clement said. "Get Mr. Wrangler some food and some hot coffee."

The Monster. A very amusing name for a fat steer. At daybreak, Wrangler rode to where he had seen it yesterday. It was not there, but its tracks were easy to follow. As he rode, he noticed the changing terrain from open woods to rocky ground. What struck Wrangler was the animal's path was not one of casual wandering, but a straight path, as if it knew exactly where it was going. It was unlikely it had ever been in these lands in its life, but its behavior spoke the opposite. But even if true, steers wouldn't be interested in rocky terrain devoid of good grazing.

He began to realize something else that was strange as he rode. The tracks indicated that it had been walking through the night. Steer don't walk around in the darkness of night—ever. And these tracks were precise, to a specific point. Wrangler started to think to himself that maybe he should leave this steer well alone—something was off. But that would never happen. He'd never leave a job unfinished, no matter how loudly his gut was telling him to do just that.

There he is.

The Monster stood in the open ground facing him. Wrangler stopped and watched it. A massive animal with a dark brown coat, short and wide, and long pointy horns. It was one fat steer. The Monster had walked to this spot for many miles in the pitch dark, with not even the moonlight to guide it. It seemed to be waiting.

Is it waiting for me?

Wrangler approached the steer, as he had done a million times before, riding up along the animal's side. He used his own horse to try to nudge the animal, but Monster wasn't having any of it. It turned to look at him with sleepy eyes and, for a moment, he thought it would fall down to sleep where it was. No amount of pushing the animal with his horse or cattle calls made Monster move.

Wrangler raced his horse away for ten yards or so, and then raced back to see if the movement would make the steer move at all, but that didn't work either. That meant he'd have to rope the fat animal and drag it along. He took the rope that was resting on his shoulder and threw the lasso around its neck.

Monster glanced at him, and, at the moment when their eyes locked on one another, Wrangler knew he had made a horrible mistake. The steer's eyes were no longer feigning sleepiness. They were showing the satisfaction of some calculating animal.

Monster bolted so fast that Wrangler was ripped off his horse. He hit the ground with a tremendous thud that rippled through his entire body and followed instantaneously by the motion of being dragged along the rocky, jagged ground. He could feel the pants of his backside and the back of his jacket being ripped to shreds. The rope had somehow managed to tangle around not only his arms, but his right leg. He was helpless to free himself, and all he could do was watch as the tragedy unfolded in slow motion.

Wrangler's eyes widened as he saw where the Monster

was dragging him. The terrain was changing again. They were headed to the edge of a cliff! The animal wasn't slowing down, but speeding up. Wrangler screamed out as he sensed that parts of his clothes on his backside were gone, and it was now his exposed skin to the ground.

The pain was so intense that he felt himself losing consciousness. He reached into his jacket with his left hand as he contracted his abs with all his might to slightly sit up. With one strike, he pounded on the rope with a curved blade. The rope was severed and he was free, but the inertia kept him sliding towards the edge. He slammed his knife's blade into the dirt and final stopped his descent over.

Wrangler couldn't be positive of what he witnessed because of the excruciating and pulsating pain in his body; and the certainty that he was gravely wounded and bleeding badly. The Monster was only a mere ten feet from him off to the side. Wrangler realized that the beast had planned to watch him slide over side unobstructed. They locked eyes again. Its expression was that of pure anger. Stopped in its tracks at the cliff's edge, it seemed to be cursing at him. A helpless Wrangler was certain the beast would charge at him, but instead, it turned its fat head and ran forward. The steer plunged off the cliff into oblivion.

A sound erupted that he had never heard in his entire existence. The falling Monster roared in fury with its bovine lungs.

Wrangler's eyes shut as he passed out.

Scotts

"There were ten of them. He was the fourth man."

Scotts hated all of them. Loathsome creatures, with their pasty white faces, bulbous noses, and all manners of colorful wigs. Their joking and comical antics were far from amusing; only one of a thousand things on his mental list that got under his skin about them. It was their ever-wiggling fingers, their exaggerated walk, and their ridiculous clothes. They were marginally acceptable in public in the daylight hours, but what about in the wee hours of night? What were they hiding with their white powdered, make-up masks? What did they do when they were alone, when no one was around to watch them closely? What evil did they engage in? Scotts hated all of them—all clowns!

Then why am I here?

He asked himself that question often. What possessed him to join the Philadelphia Circus? He needed to make a living like any other man, but he was an ex-soldier and should have been able to find some other decent and worthy work to make a living at. He should have been able to secure any one of a hundred jobs and gone an entire lifetime without ever seeing one of these loathsome creatures. He could have gone an entire lifetime without hearing the word 'clown.'

But that was the conundrum. He had special skills that were in high demand in wartime. But in peacetime, what does a man with uncanny prowess with any type of blade do? How did one make a living with battle-axes, throwing axes, and the like? A bit overqualified to be a town butcher.

"Do you think we'll get him to come again?" asked one of his circus colleagues.

"Who?"

"The President of the United States. Who else do you think I mean?"

"I don't see why not. Yes."

This new form of entertainment came to America all the way from Europe and no less than President George Washington had attended a performance. So, working in the circus was not lowly work by any means. In fact, he could make more money throwing axes at things than he could from being a soldier, a lawman, or even farming. He was stuck getting good wages by being the 'Deadly Ax-Man of Scotland' — but also having to see that clown!

Scotts continued his brief respite, drinking his ale and eating some bread off to the side. His colleagues had already moved on to get back to work. The streets were quiet, but in an hour, there would be throngs of screaming children, anxious women, and amused men queuing up for their circus extravaganza.

His expression changed to disgust as the loathsome creature appeared. When he first met Mr. McDonald, he told him straight away, "I hate clowns. I don't want to be near clowns, and since you're a clown, I don't want to be near you—ever!" His face may have been painted white and had a big smile on it, but his real smile was gone, and he probably was bright red from embarrassment under all the make-up.

That was months ago. In the beginning, McDonald would run the other way when he approached. Now, he returned the dirty looks, but always kept away. Everyone knew what the 'Deadly Ax-man of Scotland' could do with his blades, so not even Samson, their Largest Living Man in the World, would cross him.

"Go drown yourself in the pool!" Scotts yelled at him.

"Stick your axes up your..."

"Mr. McDonald!" Mrs. Tanner, one of the equestrian acrobats, yelled. Her eyes shocked at what words were about to come out of McDonald's mouth. "You are a clown. Only smiles and laughter at all times—for the children."

McDonald shot a dirty look at Scotts. Scotts laughed.

"And you, Mr. Scotts!" Mrs. Tanner yelled. "I will have words for you later. My children were better behaved than both of you."

In half an hour, his performance would begin. Scotts had his own tent, and it was larger than all the other performers combined, but no one begrudged him for it. It wasn't for sleeping, but practicing. Sometimes he'd practice his throwing techniques for six hours at a stretch. He always warmed up before a show. He could already hear a constant din from the people in and around the circus.

"Scotts!" a voice yelled from outside his tent.

Mr. Ricketts came through one of the flaps and into the tent. "You're up, my boy."

"Yes, sir." Scotts was in his costume—a dress coat with a cape and a kilt. He grabbed a long satchel from the sole table in the tent, which was filled with axes of all sizes. Two of the largest ones he carried in his right hand.

"After the show, I need you and some of the other men to do something for me." Ricketts playfully punched him in the shoulder. "It's going to be amazing!"

Mr. Ricketts obsessed about topping each show with something 'bigger and better.' He was determined for America to surpass Europe as the circus capital of the world.

"But don't think about it during your performance. Wouldn't want you to impale or decapitate the wrong person."

Ricketts burst into laughter. He frequently would set himself off in fits of laughter.

"Did I tell you how much I love you?" Ms. Fellows, the acrobat, would say before his performance.

People didn't want to see him juggle his axes, or throw them at inanimate targets, such as scarecrows. They wanted to see him throw them at a live person—missing, of course, but the closer the better. And the person with that honor was Ms. Fellows. She hid her fear perfectly and always had some romantic quip for him beforehand. Perhaps saying to herself, "He won't skewer me, if he at least likes me."

The part of the performance he hated was the 'show.' All he wanted was to do was stand, throw his axes, miss or hit whatever, recover them, bow to the audience, and go. Five minutes at the most.

"That is not showmanship, Mr. Scotts. And I don't like that name. It's not showy enough. It must scare the children, because, if you can scare the children, then you can scare the adults. Deadly Ax-man of Scotland! That's better," Mr. Ricketts had said to him the first day he joined their circus troupe. "We Scotsmen have to look out for one another."

Then Ms. Fellows and the other performers created his whole routine for him. His five minutes of performance was turned into forty minutes! Prancing about, twirling around, showing the shiny blades to the audience, and showing how sharp the blades were by chopping some large fruit or scarecrow in half, which always elicited gasps from the crowd. Then there was more prancing and twirling. Then the announcer, Mr. Ricketts, would go into the horrid background of the 'no-good Deadly Ax-man of Scotland.' This background changed from show to show, and Scotts never knew what kind of fugitive, murderer, or fugitive murderer he'd be. The women would always look at him shocked, and the children would always be giggling.

"Ladies and gentlemen, and children too, I give you the Deadly Ax-Man of Scotland, who will throw not one ax at the lovely Ms. Fellows, but, and please, I beg of you not to pass out, thirty blades!"

The gasps from the audience rumbled across the outer performance area. Mr. Ricketts was loving every moment of it. "It is a feat you have never seen before and will never see again in your whole life. And ladies and gentleman, and children too, should the unthinkable happen, should the lovely Ms. Fellows be savagely cut to pieces" — shocking gasps — "be courteous and back away from your neighbor and allow them to faint and fall to the ground, or upchuck last night's meal in peace."

Mr. Ricketts was probably bursting out laughing internally, despite his serious expression. He could see the terrified faces of the women, each wondering if they should leave immediately. All the children shifted in place to make sure they could see unobstructed, already rising on their tippy toes. The men grinned to themselves.

Scotts, without warning, marched to a large table as if he were drunk with madness and slammed it over to its side. He marched back twenty-five paces to his large satchel of weapons on the ground, threw it open, and, in a frenzy, turned and threw every ax at the table which was in front of the crowd. People screamed out; others moved away as each ax buried itself into the table. The last two weapons, giant double-axes, he lifted up above his head, yelled out, scaring even the men, and threw them down to the ground at his feet.

At this point, people were starting to wonder if this was a 'show,' or if he was mad. The crowd hadn't realized it, but they were all moving back slowly from a tight circle to an ever thinning and growing circle around the performance.

Scotts marched to the table with dozens of assorted axes sticking out of it and dragged it back to where his large double-axes were. The audience watched keenly. Scotts yelled out again, startling everyone, and started.

The first two axes sailed across the air into the wooden wall where Ms. Fellows stood in an exaggerated, carefree pose. The crowd forgot about her. The progression of his movements were so fast that it wasn't until the large double-axes were thrown, burying themselves between the spaces of Ms. Fellow's arms and hips on either side, that they grasped at what he had done. He successfully threw thirty axes at the woman in less than thirty seconds!

A few people had fainted, but the crowd erupted in applause.

"Ladies and gentlemen, and children too, the Deadly Ax-man of Scotland! The kindest man you'll ever meet!" Mr. Ricketts yelled.

The applause grew even more intense.

Forty minutes of show and now it would be an hour of 'post-show,' as Scotts called it. Every child would want to personally meet him and talk to him, their mothers would tell him how scared they were, and the men would congratulate him on a great performance.

"Look at you now," Mr. Ricketts said to him as he walked with him back to the circus office. "You're a natural. It's like you've always been the Deadly Ax-Man of Scotland."

"If you say so, Mr. Ricketts."

"I do say so, Scotts. You're a natural."

The two men entered the office, which was a temporary shack constructed at the end of the street. Inside were other circus performers, including Samson, the Largest Living Man in the World.

"What's this about, Mr. Ricketts?" one of the circus men asked.

"Men, I need you to go down to the dock and take charge of what will be the next biggest and best thing of the circus. No, it will be known as the greatest show on Earth."

"The docks?"

"You men will take charge of a large crate there and use whatever method of transportation to get it here. Take the long wagons."

"How large is this crate, Mr. Ricketts?"

"Large," he answered. "Be careful because the crate houses the newest member of our amazing troupe."

"Newest member?"

"Yes." Mr. Ricketts couldn't contain his childlike glee and smiled wide. "Mr. Simian. All the way from the magnificent, faraway lands of Timbuktu. Go on, go on. Get to the docks, get the crate, and bring Mr. Simian here."

Scotts spoke up. "Mr. Ricketts, shouldn't we do this in the morning. It's getting dark."

"Men, are you telling me you're afraid of the dark? Go on. It's not some mythical monster you're bringing back here. It's Mr. Simian, and we're not leaving him alone and hungry on the docks."

"Hungry? Mr. Ricketts…what does Mr. Simian eat for food?"

Mr. Ricketts looked at him and then burst out laughing. "Go on," he managed to say. "Mr. Simian doesn't eat people." He laughed more. "Mr. Simian is an herbivore." Ricketts bent over, his stomach was hurting from the intensity of his laughter.

"You heard Mr. Ricketts," Samson said. "Let's go get Mr. Simian."

"Hey, where's McDonald?" another performer asked.

"Forget him," Scotts interjected. "We don't need him."

The men rode the long wagon through the nearly empty streets, two on the driver's seat and the rest bouncing around in the long, open wagon being pulled along by four large Shire horses.

The circus always set-up on the outskirts of town. During the day, they attracted a good crowd from all parts, near and far, but at night the indigenous people that lived nearby were usually of the less than savory class.

It didn't take all that long to reach the docks. Two dock workers waited, each holding a lantern, but from the look on their faces, the circus group surmised that they were expected earlier.

"Are you with the circus?" one of the dock men called out in an impatient voice.

"Yes," Samson answered back as they slowed the long wagon to a complete stop.

"You are lucky gentlemen as we were about to leave. You were supposed to have been here three hours ago. Everyone is gone. The only reason we're here is because we couldn't leave some wild animal on the dock. It might get out into the public or someone might happen upon it and let it out."

"We apologize, sir. We didn't know we were supposed to be here sooner."

"Well, let's get on with it."

The dock men led them closer to the docks where a couple of ships were anchored. The docks, the streets, and the surrounding area were a virtual ghost town with not another person anywhere to be seen.

"This area is spooky at night," one of the circus men said.

One of the dock men gave a look and pointed. "There's your shipment."

The men expected to see a large crate, but what the dock man pointed to was massive—no less than eight feet by eight feet in dimensions.

"Sir, this cannot be the proper crate," Samson said.

"It is the proper crate," the dock man answered and looked at his notebook, squinting his eyes to read. "Yes, for Mr. John B. Ricketts of the Rickett's Circus. Straight from Transylvania."

"Transylvania?" one of the men asked. "The shipment is supposed to be from Timbuktu."

"What difference does that make? Both start with the letter T. Someone wrote it wrong. It happens all the time."

"Those two words are nothing alike," Scotts said. "This is the wrong crate."

"This is the right crate," the dock man corrected with a huff. "It has the name of the right party, and who else would have a wild animal in a crate. It's yours, and we insist you take charge of your shipment and be quick about it."

The circus men looked at one another.

"If you have any complaints, you should have been here three hours ago when you were supposed to be. I need one of you to sign for the shipment." He pushed another paper into Samson's face to sign.

Samson wasn't pleased, but scribbled something legible on it. The dock man looked at it, made a sound, folded it, and then put it in his notebook.

"Gentlemen, have a good night."

With that, the two dock men walked away and disappeared into the night.

"What do we do now?" one of the circus men asked. "We can lift the thing, but it looks like it's too heavy for the wagon."

"We don't know that," Samson said. "It looks heavy,

but maybe it's not heavy at all. Let's check the weight. We can lift up one side and see."

The men watched Samson. He rubbed his hands together and walked to the massive crate. He was about to lift one side of it when he stopped. Samson put his ear to the crate.

"We haven't heard a sound yet," he said.

"Maybe Mr. Simian is sleeping. Don't monkeys sleep a lot?"

"Where is Transylvania? I never heard of the place."

"Eastern Europe," Scotts answered. "The whole region is a dreary place."

"Europe is a dreary place," the man said back.

"Do they have monkeys there?" another man asked.

Scotts thought to himself. "Actually, I never heard of monkeys living there, but they have wooded areas."

"Why would Mr. Ricketts get a monkey from Eastern Europe? That's not exotic. That's stupid. He was getting animals from Africa and the Far East. Scotts is right. This is the wrong crate."

"Let's get it into the wagon and back to the circus and sort it out with Mr. Ricketts," Samson said as he bent his knees and slowly lifted one side of the crate off the ground. He smiled. "The crate isn't that heavy."

Scotts moved to the crate and pressed his ear to it. He snapped his head back in shock as he stepped back from it.

"What's wrong, Scotts?"

A savage scream erupted from inside the crate so loud that Samson fell to the ground, startled, and every man jumped.

Two of the circus men ran away to the long wagon as fast as they could.

"Get back here!" Samson yelled as he got back to his feet. "It's in the crate. We're not in any danger."

Suddenly, they heard a melee of pounding from inside the crate and the wooden crate started to crack.

The rest of the circus men looked at one another and then ran. They quickly reached the long wagon as the first two men were already beginning to drive the wagon away. Samson and Scotts were the last to jump into the wagon.

Another animal scream ripped through the night, louder and more ferocious than before. *It was out of the crate!*

The horses needed no prompting to run faster. They were more frightened than the men and bolted. The men stared back at the dock, praying that they did not see anything.

"Scotts, what did you hear inside before it screamed?"

Scotts looked at his colleague with a pained face. "When we get back to safety I'll say."

"Look!" one of the men yelled.

A giant black, hairy shape was running after them on all fours.

"Ride faster!" Samson yelled to the drivers.

"We must stop it!" Scotts yelled.

The men watched in disbelief as the Scotsman leaped out of the wagon. He fell, rolled his body to a stop on the dirt road, and then stood to his feet.

"He has his weapons," said one of the men.

"He does?"

"I saw the reflection of the blade."

They couldn't stop the horses, even if they wanted to. Another hellish animal scream echoed through the night.

Scotts stood in the middle road with a double-ax in each hand, waiting, ignoring the pain of his fall, and slightly hyperventilating. He stared in the direction of the animal's scream, but saw nothing appear in the night. He slowed his breathing and concentrated on listening for even the slightest sound around him. Then he heard it—the heavy breathing of something out of sight, but he knew it was stalking him. Scotts ran.

He ran as fast as he could, but continuously threw his head back to check behind him. His hands were tense, ready to strike anything that came at him. He could sense the animal. It was there. It was toying with him.

There was no way for him to tell how much time had passed, but he knew he had been running for a while. Incredulously, he now realized that he had run all the way back. The location of the circus was in sight.

Did I really run so far?

The fact seemed unbelievable to him, as he had never been a good runner over distances—and he was running with a large ax in each hand. *Does fear really make you capable of superhuman feats?* It took their wagon, pulled by four powerful horses, more than a half hour to travel the distance and now here he was—

The animal pounced on him from high above with such intensity that he was thrown through the air and crashed into the wall of a nearby building several feet away. He hit upside down and slid, crashing on the very top of his head, and piled over. He was so disoriented that it took him a few moments to become aware that the animal was literally ripping him apart with his claws. He felt its hot breath as it neared him again, its mouth wide enough to bite his face off.

Scotts reflexively reacted. Miraculously, his hands had remained locked in a death grip on his weapons and he slashed wildly at the animal. It screamed, and the sound rippled through his body, but his arms never stopped their attacks. He was slicing his simian attacker to pieces.

Despite his near-conscious state, he somehow managed to stand. He stumbled back and collapsed backwards to the ground. An unnatural sensation began to wash over his body and he knew it was the beginnings of death. He was glad it was dark, because if he saw the wounds that the animal inflicted on him, he would have probably died from the sight of it alone. He lay on the ground and stared up at the stars waiting for it to happen—death.

An upside face came into his view, looking down at him. The pasty white face and bulbous red nose. Mr. McDonald grabbed him under his armpits and dragged him back to the circus.

Scotts looked up at him, his mind filled with only repentant thoughts. *I will never be mean to him again if I live.*

The animal's unholy patron could never have anticipated that a clown would have saved the man's life that night.

The Bully Boys

"There were ten of them. They were the fifth and sixth men. I like them."

The town of Pride boasted to all of its peace and quiet. Today, however, people screamed and ran from the violence within. The pandemonium was solely the work of two brutes of men who brawled in the center of Main Street.

One man was taller than the other, but both men were huge; their bodies were a combination of bulky muscle and fat—visible to all, as they had ripped off their tops when they began brawling. The shorter man had a droopy left eye, and both men had missing teeth. The tall one, with a scar across his right cheek, punched the short one down to the ground. The short one got up to his feet and charged him like a bull, slamming into him and pushing him back towards the wall of one of the businesses. They both smashed right through the wall.

Townspeople gathered at each end of the street to watch them. Their distressed faces looked at one another, not knowing what to do.

"These mad men have to be stopped. They'll destroy our town," one man said.

"Who's going to stop them?" another asked. "No one here."

The two brutes emerged from the hole in the wall, laughing hysterically. The short one slapped the larger one on the back as they both walked back to the tavern where their fight had started.

A man ran down the street to them and yelled, "That's my place of business! You're going to pay for that damage! What do you have to say for yourselves?"

The men laughed at him. The tall one walked up to the man and punched him square in the face; the owner collapsed cold to the ground.

The two brutes laughed even louder and continued walking to the tavern. When they arrived, the place was empty of any customers, except for the owner who glared at them.

"Get out of my place of business this instant, you two maniacs! You scared away all my customers."

The two men laughed at him.

"How much business do you even do in this worthless town? Your food is feces and your ale is piss."

"Get out!" the tavern owner yelled again.

The tall one reached into his pocket and pulled out some coins. He looked at them in his hand and then threw them at the owner, who ducked.

"Go! Get out of here before we beat the teeth out of your face and the brains out of your head. Get," the tall brute commanded.

The tavern owner came out from behind the main counter and ran out of the place.

The short man looked at his comrade, grinned mischievously, and then ran behind the counter. He bent down and began to place every empty mug from the shelves on the counter. Laughing, he filled every last one with ale and then began drinking each one empty.

"Fool," the tall one said to him. "You drink like a fish."

The droopy-eyed man stopped drinking for a moment, and then refilled every mug again. He began to guzzle each one again, laughing and burping along the way.

The tavern owner appeared from the back door and his eyes widened in shock.

"What are you doing? Stop drinking all of my stock!"

The tall man picked up one the chairs and threw it at him. The chair broke apart upon impact, smashing the poor man to the ground. He got up on his knees first, looking like he wanted to cry, and then got to his feet.

Droopy-Eyes continued to guzzle the mugs of ale and stopped to throw one of them at the owner. The glass barely missed the man's head, and, with that, the owner ran out of the tavern again.

A cowboy rode up the road of the large Livingstone Ranch. He stopped the horse, jumped off, and ran into the large house, past a man standing guard next to the door.

Mr. Livingstone sat at the table of his outside patio eating lunch with several of his men. He smoked his pipe, dressed in a black suit.

"Mr. Livingstone!" The cowboy ran out of the house to him.

The man looked up at him and the other men turned around.

"Mr. Livingstone, they're back!"

"Who's back?"

"Those two lunatics. They're in town. Your town, sir. They're destroying it."

The boss jumped up from the table with a look of anger. "Get everyone from inside! We're going to end this once and for all."

"Should we pay the money we owe them? That's what this is all about."

The boss stopped to glower at him. "I'm paying them nothing. But I will toss a few coins on their tombstones when this is done."

The town inn was ablaze, and the two Bully Boys stood in front of it, still topless and laughing hysterically. It was the second building they had destroyed in town—the tavern they had torn down with their bare hands after drinking all the alcohol.

The posse arrived with their boss in the lead. The two brutes saw them and stopped laughing. Instead, they smiled with great satisfaction.

The riders surrounded the Bully Boys.

"I told you two never to come back here again or I'd kill you."

"We told you that no one steals from us," the tall one said.

"No one," the shorter one added.

"I'm going to do a lot worse than that, as you will soon find out," Livingstone said.

The shorter Bully Boy, Droopy-Eyes, looked up at one of the riders. "Come here!" He pulled the man down from his horse and threw him to the ground. Before the rider could get up, the brute stomped down on his neck with both feet. Everyone heard the snap.

Livingstone yelled, "Kill them!"

The Bully Boys laughed. Scar punched Livingstone's horse in the head, and the animal reared up, throwing Livingstone off its back. Droopy-Eye grabbed two more men from their horses and preceded to beat both men to death.

All the other riders scattered as Scar threw the full weight of his body onto a helpless Livingstone on the ground.

The riders gathered together at the end of the street and watched their boss being savagely beaten by both Bully Boys.

"We must stop them. There's only two of them," one of the posse said.

"Let's run them down with the horses," another said.

"Yes. Stampede them."

The men lined up and charged with their horses. Scar waited where he stood, smiling, but Droopy-Eye yelled out and ran to them. The riders didn't flinch even as Droopy-Eye stretched out his arms and jumped, knocking two men off their horses.

"Run that one down!" one of the riders directed as they ignored their two fallen riders and raced at the other Bully Boy.

The lead rider was riding as fast as he could, but Scar didn't react until the last possible moment. He jumped up and snatched the shocked man from his horse. Scar ran a few feet and jumped again to punch another rider off his horse.

"You animal!" one of the riders said as he stopped his horse in front of Scar and drew his weapon.

He never got to shoot. Something hit him from behind and he fell from the horse. All he heard was loud crying as he rolled over to see a small boy next to him crying his eyes out.

"What! You threw a little boy at me! I can't believe it. What kind of cruel animal are you?"

The rider furiously tried to get at his pistol again, but Droopy-Eye was on top of him, running extremely fast for his size.

"Come here!" the Bully Boy said, reaching out both hands for him.

"No!" the rider dropped his pistol and scrambled away before he could get caught.

A woman appeared from nowhere and lunged at Droopy-Eye, scratching his face. He laughed and punched her, sending her crashing to the ground. The little boy, cried even louder, but got up and ran to his mother, instinctively covering her with his body. He looked up at the laughing brute.

"You!" a voice called out and Scar turned around.

One of the fallen riders plunged a knife into his chest.

The two men stared at each other for a while. The rider expected to see the brute yell out, cry, something, but his only reaction was to smile and then start laughing. The rider backed away from him in fear, looking at the knife. It was embedded in the Bully Boy's chest, and he was bleeding, but Scar was not reacting as a normal person would.

"You're not human."

Scar pulled the knife from his chest, wiped the blood off on his face, and pointed at the rider. "Let me try now."

"Stop! Stop! Tell us what you want to make you both

stop, go away, and never come back."

"You stole from us!" Scar pointed the knife at him again.

"If we give you the money, will you go?"

"Double what we are owed!"

"I will get it for you if you stop." The rider looked at all the remaining riders. "Stop! Everyone stop! Come over here now!"

"They killed the boss," said one of the men.

"And five of our men," said another.

"Stop the fighting!"

The Bully Boys put their shirts and coats back on as they grinned at the remaining men, with their new cloth bag of cash in Scar's hand.

"We would have destroyed the entire town, came out to your ranch and burnt it out, and then hunted you all down 'til we caught up to you and killed you. No one steals from us," Scar said.

"No one," Droopy-Eye echoed.

"Leave now and never come back."

"We would never have come to your filthy town the first time, if you didn't hire us. Was it worth it? Trying to double-cross us out of the money you owed us, was it worth it?"

"Obviously, it wasn't," the rider answered. "Go."

"You get on the wrong side of the Bully Boys and we make sure you wish you were never born. Nothing alive can defeat us when we set our evil eye against you."

"Please go."

"Next time you hire someone to do a job, you better pay them for the job done. The next person may not be as charitable as Droopy-Eye and me. They might just cut you all down with no show of mercy."

"Please go."

"That's how Droopy-Eye and me got started. We would find the local bully who preyed on the weak and beat them up, sometimes beat them to death. No one is more powerful than us."

"You have your money, please go."

"You people think you rule the world. Take advantage of simple folks. Never! try to steal from someone again. We should stay and teach you a lesson."

The riders remained quiet. They prayed the Bully Boys would simply go.

"Lucky for all of you, we hate this place."

"Hate it," Droopy-Eyes added.

The Bully Boys eyed the men a final time, cursing at them under their breath, and then walked to where their horses waited. They mounted their horses and rode.

The town watched them go, careful not to outwardly show the utter contempt and hatred they felt for the brutes. The Bully Boys rode out and disappeared over the ridge.

"Look over there," Droopy-Eyes said, looking behind them. "I'm sure it's the same man following us again."

They were only two miles from Pride. A lone figure in the distance was at the top of a large hill.

"Who could it be?" Scar asked.

"Should we ride after him?"

"No. Why worry over one man, whoever he is. We'll get him in the next town if we see him again. Let's get stronger, faster horses to replace these ones. We can get him then."

"Yes. Get him then. He's never on horseback though."

"We never see him on horseback, but he can't move around so fast without a horse. Must be hiding it."

"Must be. But we'll get him in the next town."

"Beat him into the ground. Perhaps drag him a few miles or so from the horse for fun."

The Bully Boys started to laugh as they rode on.

It patiently watched the two men ride off. Its face hidden by the hooded cloak it wore. It had followed them for months to learn their habits and weaknesses. It had prepared and fantasized about the encounter all the time. It was more than ready, but the master had changed his mind.

The wind blew its hood back a bit. As the dust cyclone came in fast, its body crumbled down into the barren ground and was gone.

Morgan

"There were ten of them. He was the seventh man."

Morgan came riding over the bluff to them, in no particular hurry at all. Their cabin homes were all within sight of each other. The men were gathered together, thirty strong, with their muskets and pistols. The women were all together with the children in the center home, and a few of them were armed, too. It was the Thomas boy who had seen the stranger first.

He kept his hands on his reins, making no threatening movements as he slowly approached.

"This new American government doesn't seem all that different from the one we overthrew," their leader said to them as they watched him. "With the stroke of a pen, telling us our land, the entire Ohio Territory, everything west of the Appalachians, belongs to them and not the people who have slaved over it day and night to make a home with their families."

"We defended it from the British and the Indians. We can defend it from you and your United States," one of the men said.

"These government land grabbers in Philadelphia may get themselves another revolution, if they don't mind themselves," the leader added.

As the man drew near on his pale, gray horse, they could see him clearly. All dark-colored clothes and a hat that seemed to be the exact color and shade of his horse. At first they thought he was a fat man, but then realized that he was wearing clothes that were about two sizes too big.

"Good day gentlemen. My name is … "Morgan began.

"Save your words stranger," said one man. "We know who you are, government man."

"Good. I hate when people pretend not to know what's going on and I have to recite all kinds of official declarations and judgments."

"What might we do for you?" The man who spoke stood in the center of the group. He exuded a demeanor of command—probably an ex-officer in the War.

"Is this how you welcome everyone who happens upon you?"

"This is how we welcome trespassers."

"Trespassers? How can someone trespass on land that is not yours?"

"Stranger, this land belongs to us because we're the ones who settled it, live upon it, built our homes here, tend our crops here, and raise our families here. No one was here when we got here, and now that we are here, lots of people want to steal it from us." The man gripped his musket tightly. "The Indians came here to chase off, a few different tribes, but we are still here, and they are not. We fought one war to throw off the tyranny of King George, only to get King Washington. This is our land, and no kings or presidents or Indians or anyone else will take it from us."

Morgan sat listening to the man with a sour look and his arms folded.

"As for you and your bunch of squatters," —that word drew words of anger from the men—"the law of the land says the Ohio Territory is under the jurisdiction of the United States of America, and this land belongs to others who have purchased it."

"Purchased it?" The man laughed, as did the other men. "How can a man purchase a piece of Earth created by the Almighty?"

"I did not come here to argue the law with you, only to tell you what you have to do, all of you."

"We are thirty armed men, and behind us are armed women. We don't recognize your authority, trespasser. Turn your scurvy horse around, and go back to wherever you came from."

"Don't make me become violent."

"What are you going to do when you are one against thirty?"

The stranger drew pistols from beneath his jacket, one in each hand. He shot at their leader with one pistol, and then reached into his jacket again, as the pistol fell to the ground, and fired with the other hand. He shot with a new gun as the other hand dropped its pistol to draw a fourth gun. The effect was their leader had a steady stream of bullets fly around his body as every other man backed away, and the stranger's pistols from his jacket piled up on the ground. All while the leader yelled a steady repetition of "No!" "No!" "No!"

The stranger stopped. "Drop that musket!" he yelled.

The leader did so.

"All of you!"

All the men dropped their weapons.

"My name is Morgan, and I am a duly appointed agent of the government. You are trespassers by law. If you feel you are being wronged, then do what everyone else does. Get a lawyer and take your case before the proper authorities. What you don't do is take up arms against official agents of the government. What if the government decided to send the Army in after you with three hundred men? What would you do then? They'd pack you all up, those they didn't shoot dead, and throw you off the land, and then where would you be?"

"We want you people to leave us alone!" the leader yelled at him. "We came here when no one else would, and we made it our home before it was ever part of America! How can two men far away, by writing on a piece a paper, suddenly say we have no claim to our own land?"

"Mister, when you lose a war, you don't get to make the rules."

"Lose a war? What do you mean?"

"You're British loyalists?"

"That is nonsense. We're Americans. We want to be left alone! British, French, American, Indian. Leave us alone!"

Morgan looked at the man and at the other men, confused.

"What do you intend to do, mister? I doubt you have thirty more pistols in that jacket to shoot at us again," said another man.

Before he could bend down to the ground to grab his musket, Morgan began his melee of shooting again. The leader, and the other men this time, ran away to the closest cabin as their unfortunate comrade closed his eyes and froze in place as bullets flew by his head.

Morgan stopped shooting. The man slowly opened his eyes and saw an even larger pile of pistols on either side of the stranger's horse. He didn't wait; he turned around and ran away into the cabin to join the others.

"Now that you all are unarmed, perhaps we can talk like adults, and no one gets killed."

He got down from his horse and gathered up his pile of weapons. His jacket was made with special pockets to carry dozens of pistols at a time. He had them specially made to be smaller than the normal one-shot pistol.

As he kicked all their weapons together in a pile, he noticed someone approaching in the distance, coming across the plain. It was a tiny woman dressed in black. He kept an eye on her and the cabin of the squatters. The cabin door opened and their leader appeared, looking at the approaching woman. Soon, other men, and a few women, stepped outside near the door to watch her too.

"I was told you were on the side of the British," Morgan said to them.

"That's nonsense," the leader said. "I was a major in the Continental Army. How could you not know that? How could King Washington not know that?"

Morgan smirked. "Obviously, the new American government wants Americans to stay on this land, more to follow, and even more to move West. There are thirteen states today. There's no reason we can't have many more in the years to come. Petition the government and get your legal papers to be here legal."

"What do you intend to do, mister government agent,

because we don't care about any of that? We just want to be left alone."

"I can see you're not the reasonable type."

"No, we're not."

"Are you planning on causing me any trouble? Because no one has gotten injured or killed, to this point."

"The day is still young, mister," the leader said, but he was not looking at Morgan.

"Who is that woman?" Morgan also stared at the woman.

"Why should I help you?"

"Because the Almighty would want you to."

"That's funny coming from a heathen like you."

"The Almighty made heathens too."

"True, but I still feel no generosity towards a man who intends to take my family's home to give away to greedy, government land barons far away from here. That's why we left the colonies."

"They're states now, not colonies. And the government has no interest in this land. Why aren't you listening to me? The government wants to see Americans settle it far and wide."

"I hear the talk, but not the sincerity."

"For an ex-officer who served under Washington in the Army, you don't sound like you're grateful that we won. You sound like you wanted to remain as slaves under the Crown."

The leader scoffed. "I fought for the freedom of men to control their own destiny, from the British or anyone else, even those in Philadelphia. What were you fighting for?"

Morgan smirked. Both men were watching the woman again.

The woman was no more than fifteen feet away from them. She was under five-feet in height and looked more like a moving doll than a person.

"Why are you scared of this woman? Who is she?"

"You will find out presently."

The woman walked right up to Morgan, so close that she was almost touching. Her head tilted up to look directly into his eyes as he stared down at her. He was six feet tall but felt extremely nervous.

"Can I help you, ma'am?"

"You must accompany me," she said.

"Why?" Morgan heard a noise and turned his head. The leader was gone. The noise was the cabin door closing shut. The door locked, and not one of them was looking through the windows.

"Because you must."

"To do what?"

"To help me. I was told of your arrival, and you must accompany me so you can help us."

"Us?"

"Yes, me and him."

"Your husband?"

The woman smiled, and all Morgan could see was rotting teeth and blackened gums.

"Yes, you can say the master is my husband."

"The master?"

"You must accompany me. Dealing with these people is beneath you. They are never going to leave, and you will not harm them. You are wasting time. Your purpose is elsewhere. I must introduce you to the people who do matter."

"Ma'am, who are you?"

"My name is unimportant. All that is important is you, the others, and the master."

Morgan felt his conversation with the woman was the equivalent of a stationery cyclone—endlessly revolving in circles, but going nowhere.

"You are a good man," she said. "I am an old woman. The people here are mean and cruel to me. I would leave but I have no place to go. My husband is bedridden, and I cannot manage anymore. You could help us; take us to the next town. I do not have much money, but we will give you all that we have. We deserve a better life too. We may not be smart or youthful or have means, but we deserve a better life. Will you help us? Rescue my husband and I from those that can harm us? We have no one else to turn to."

Morgan sighed. She was probably crazy, but, at the moment, she looked helpless and worthy of pity.

"It's not far away," she added. "You saw me walk here. I am not a strong woman." As if she anticipated his coming question, she said, "I saw you ride in as they did. I had to take the chance that you were a good man. I see that you are. The master was right. I mean, my husband was right."

"How far away exactly?"

"Over the ridge." She pointed. "Not more than two miles."

"I suppose you want me to take you on horseback."

"Oh no, you can follow me." The woman didn't wait for him to answer and started walking back the way she came.

Who was this woman? he asked himself.

He mounted his horse and glanced at the cabin. He

could swear there were dozens of faces watching from the windows, but they were now gone. The entire home seemed deserted, though there were at least forty people crammed inside.

Morgan rode behind the tiny woman at a steady pace. She looked like she was walking at the same speed as before, but they reached the ridge much faster. As they went over the ridge, he looked back at the cabin and saw the figures of dozens of people watching them. His horse was over the ridge now and the view was gone.

Ahead in the distance, along the nearly barren plains, was what looked to be a small shack near the edge of a cliff.

"It is beautiful there, especially when you watch the sun rise in the mornings and set in the evening."

Again, she anticipated a thought he had in his head but had not said aloud.

"Is your husband very ill?"

"He is. Few people understand him, that's why we have to protect him. All of us in our own way."

"There's more than the two of you?"

"Not here. I am the only one here for him. As a good man yourself, you know that sometimes people will come along and try to upset the balance of nature; try to harm the way things have always been. It shocks me, personally, that this happens and these people exist. There is no reason for it. You understand, don't you? The harm that could come must be prevented before it can ever manifest."

They had reached the shack. It was a small, rotting structure, and Morgan wondered how human beings could live in such a wretched domicile.

"This is what we have been reduced to, kind sir. We no longer have the means or the physical strength to keep up our home." She pushed the door open and disappeared into the dark of the shack's interior.

Morgan dismounted slowly and stood next to his horse. He felt uneasy.

The woman suddenly ran out in a panic.

"No, he is gone! He is not here!"

The woman's hands were shaking as she grasped at her mouth and face. Morgan looked down to the ground and saw tracks that looked like someone or something was dragged, or was dragging himself, from the shack's interior towards the cliff's edge. She noticed the signs too.

"He cannot see well. He went off the cliff! Please, I cannot lose him. He is my life."

"Wait here, ma'am." Morgan hadn't even finished his sentence when the woman dashed off towards the cliff's edge.

He ran after her. They neared the edge of the cliff and he could hear the torrent of the river waters over its side. The woman frantically looked around as she kept running. Morgan ran faster and grabbed her shoulder. He was overcome by a sickening feeling as he slowly removed his hand—her shoulder felt like fragile, but sharp, miniaturized bone.

"Stay back, ma'am," he said to her as he gestured for her to stand still, and he turned to look over the cliff.

He jutted his neck over to see what he could see. It was not a sheer drop. The cliff dropped down about ten feet and then sloped down into the moving waters.

"Ma'am, I don't see him."

A gust of unnatural winds came upon him suddenly.

He tucked his head as he closed his eyes tight.

Morgan felt something push him—his eyes popped open wide—and he careened over the edge. He yelled out as he fell. He expected to hit the ground, roll down the hill, and fall the rest of the way into the cold water but, ten feet down, he crashed through the ground into a hole of darkness.

He landed about six feet below. Stunned, he remained still until he could collect his wits. His entire body began to ache, and some parts were throbbing with intense pain. At first, he thought the pain was making his skin tingle, but he realized in horror that his skin was not crawling with pain. *Something was crawling over his skin.*

Morgan screamed as he felt his body swarmed over by an army of insects. He wasn't able to see them, despite the daylight beaming through the hole, which only intensified his terror. He thrashed around with his right arm, his left one was pinned by something, and when he touched his face, he could feel their tiny crawling bodies, hundreds of them. His screaming was hysterical, and he flailed around in a mad panic to get the insects off of him.

Then he saw her. The tiny woman stood from the ledge watching him with a black smile on her face. *And he saw her master.* He was convinced he had succumbed to madness—her companion was a moving skeleton, standing next to her as if it was the most normal thing in the world.

The insects felt as if they were eating him alive! He went mad and reached into his jacket, drew and fired.

The bullet hit her in the forehead. *She fell from the ledge above.* Her body crashed through the sinkhole and on top of him. He screamed. His left arm was freed by whatever had pinned it in the dark, and he crawled over her dead body and out of the sinkhole. He kept crawling along the ground and saw the infestation—hundreds of fist-sized spiders over his entire body, some crawling over his open eyes. Morgan jumped up to his feet, ran frantically, virtually falling down the slope for twenty feet, and jumped into the icy river rapids.

Shaunessy

"There were ten of them. He was the eighth man."

The young man was getting a headache from the busyness of the place. He waited his turn until the seaman could attend to him.

"Flynn Shaunessy is my name."

"Destination?"

"The United States."

"Are you American?"

Shaunessy gave him a quizzical look. "With this accent?"

"I have no ear for accents."

"Irish. I'm an Irishman."

"The dark complexion of your skin says you must have come from an exotic land or two."

"I have."

"Do you mind if I ask where you plan to visit in the new United States?"

"A place called Sleepy Hollow."

The seaman looked at him and smiled. "I haven't heard that town's name in years. Do you know its ill-reputation?

A haunted town with a headless horseman?"

"The same."

"Trading in exotic adventures for haunted ones. Let's hope you don't meet any headless horseman, real or imaginary."

"Actually, my intent is to meet this headless horseman face-to-face, in a manner of speaking. We have some serious business to attend to together."

The man was no longer smiling. "You can board now, sir. Over there, the captain will help you." He was no longer interested in having anything to do with the man.

"Thank you."

Lisbon, Portugal was a beautiful city but he was eager to get on his way. The transatlantic ship was the largest vessel he had ever seen in his life, but the journey would be far from comfortable or safe.

Shaunessy should not have been apprehensive about the prospect of being on the open seas again, but he was. The trip to America would take over a month, almost two; the end of his two-year journey from his small hometown in Ireland, to the Far East, and back to Europe. Now, he settled in his chair on the lounge area of the ship's deck headed for America. He would either return to his native country from there, or he would die in America. He didn't fool himself about the stakes.

Cooped up on a large ship with a myriad of strangers for weeks—his body shuddered for a moment at the thought. He was a land-lover to the core. Though he felt that watching the seas would keep his mind from the true danger of his quest ahead. It was not a casual sightseeing endeavor. It would be a battle for his life and soul.

"Is this seat taken, young man?"

Shaunessy looked up to see a distinguished, well-dressed gentleman standing next to him.

"Not at all. Please."

"Thank you kindly."

The man had a small blanket draped over one shoulder, and he held a small leather bag in his other hand. He settled himself in the chair, kept his bag close, and wrapped himself in the blanket.

"It can get as nippy as a London night, even at noon, on these ships. They can build these modern wonders of sea-going transportation but can't seem to figure out how to keep a man even moderately warm. "

Shaunessy smiled. "Indeed."

"The name's Henry Horrace."

"Flynn Shaunessy."

"Nice to meet you. What fine country do you hail from? I hear the accent."

"The Great Kingdom of Ireland."

"Of course. Myself, well, I already revealed I'm from Great Britain. Is this your first trip out of Europe?"

"My second."

"Where was the first?"

"To the Far East."

"Ahh, whereabouts exactly?"

"China."

"Ahh, I have been there myself. Amazing country. I've been many places—Middle East, Africa, America—but I think nothing tantalized me more than when I was in Great China. Was it business or pleasure?"

"Business."

"Very good. It's always best when you can get someone else to pay for your travel."

"Indeed, but, in my case, I did have to handle all the expenses myself. I had to work my way there with an endless string of jobs. I am, by no means, wealthy."

"As someone who is, I can only sum up its life with one word: boredom. My evil brood of no-good children would obviously disagree, but I have a surprise for them. If it is a matter of happiness and wealth, choose happiness. I made that mistake once. Could have married my childhood sweetheart, but I had to become a man of means and let her go. Over a half a century later that decision haunts me daily. I chose wealth over happiness. Never do it. You have children, Mr. Shaunessy?"

"None, as of yet."

"Hurry up, hurry up. Have them when you're young. That's the best way."

"You said you had a surprise for your children."

Mr. Horrace laughed and then leaned over to him. "My no-good children, all five of them, are waiting with baited breath for my demise and inevitable crossing over to the after-life so they can inherit all my money." He laughed again. "They have no idea I left them a grand total of ten pounds each, and that's it. My entire fortune I've willed to my loyal servants. I wish I could impose on God to allow me just a mere few moments to gaze down to see the shocked expressions on their faces when my will is read."

"Funny."

"When I die, they'll bury me in America—right next to my late wife. Otherwise, my no-good children would deface my tombstone." He leaned back. "But enough of them. Do tell me, what made you travel to Great China?"

"I would rather not say, but … I had to see if a rumor was true or not about something I was looking for."

"Was it true?"

"It was."

"Yes, it's an amazing country. The history, the locales, the people. If you were looking for something that you'd find no other place in the world, then it would no doubt be there. Where are you headed to in America, Mr. Shaunessy?"

"New York."

He could see the man was waiting for him to say more.

"Sleepy Hollow."

Mr. Horrace slapped his leg with a smile. "Sleepy Hollow and the Headless Horseman. You have a definite sense of adventure, Mr. Shaunessy. Have you ever been there before?"

"I've never been to America before. I have a sister and brother there who have kept me informed over the years."

"Are you going there to see if you can see some ghosts?" Mr. Horrace asked with a grin.

"I'm going there to see if can kill me one."

Mr. Horrace looked at him with some confusion. "You can't kill a ghost, Mr. Shaunessy. You can cast them out, but that's about all."

"I wonder though."

"Mr. Shaunessy, you seem to be a righteous and intelligent man. I get the impression you are wondering about things you shouldn't and acting upon them."

"How can you guess all that?"

"Are you on this quest of yours alone?"

"I am. My father always told me that when something needs to be done right, then you need to do it yourself."

"Where's your father now?"

"He's … He's dead."

Mr. Horrace hesitated for a moment. "I'm sorry to hear that, young man. Where did he meet his end?"

Shaunessy looked at Mr. Horrace and knew that he didn't even have to answer. The man had already pieced it together. "Sleepy Hollow."

"Mr. Shaunessy, then your next action upon your immediate arrival in America is clear. Slow down what you're doing and get help. Your father's words are correct, but you are misapplying them to this situation. When a man goes into battle, it is always better to have a man on your left, a man on your right, and a man at your back."

Shaunessy reflected for a moment.

"If our places were reversed, I wouldn't set foot near Sleepy Hollow until that was accomplished. I would tell you to get off this ship right now and don't even go, but I know that's never going to happen. Therefore, I give you that as my next best advice."

"I appreciate that, sir."

"Good. I can tell you all about my own travels around the world. It's sometimes hard to find the right companion on these long trips to pass the time. I certainly received my share of luck this time."

Shaunessy smiled.

"May I ask you to do an old man a favor? With my frail body, I can only manage to carry one of my cases, but I have another. It's with the attendants on the dock. Can you fetch it for me? I'm sure he's there now, but he wasn't when I arrived, and I had to get off these old legs. Unlike my no-good children would do, I always spend as little as possible when I travel. No large entourage of servants for me. My vacations are to get away from everyone."

"I can do that." Shaunessy stood from his chair.

"Here. Put my smaller case in the chair to make sure no one takes it."

Shaunessy placed the light bag on the chair.

"Thank you, Mr. Shaunessy. I wish I had a son like you instead of my no-good children."

Shaunessy laughed and headed back to the gangplank. He moved through arriving passengers, both rich and poor, and everything in between. All were walking up the gangplank and he was the only one going the other way. He brushed past a young woman who smiled at him. Shaunessy stepped down to the dock and watched her disappear before turning around to find a ship crewman.

As he walked to the man, he stopped at the sight of a set of bags clustered together — they were his bags.

Shaunessy ran to the seaman. "Excuse me."

"Yes, sir?"

"Those bags." He pointed. "Why aren't they on the ship? They were loaded on and now they're not."

The seaman looked at them. "Who are you, sir?"

"I'm Flynn Shaunessy and bound for America on this ship."

"Come with me."

The seaman led him to the ship's captain who had the passenger manifest in his hand.

"Do you have a Flynn Shaunessy on the passenger list?"

The other man looked down the list.

"You checked me in, sir, yourself. Don't you remember?"

The man looked up and studied his face. "Oh yes. I do, but your man came back and had us remove your luggage."

"Excuse me," Shaunessy said. "My man? I'm traveling alone. Why would I have my luggage removed?"

"Your man said you'd catch the next ship to America."

"My man? I have no man. Next ship to America?" Shaunessy was getting angry. "Please return my luggage back to the ship. I'm taking this ship."

"Sir, your man not only had your luggage removed for the next passage to America, but paid for the passage."

"Paid?" Shaunessy shook his head. "I don't understand. What did the man look like?"

The Captain described Shaunessy's man in full detail—he had described Mr. Horrace.

Shaunessy's face was red with anger.

"Is that your man or not?" the Captain asked.

"This person is playing some kind of prank on me."

"You know this person?"

"Yes. He introduced himself to me as a Mr. Horrace."

The two ship's employees looked at each other then back at him.

"What's wrong?"

"A Mr. Horrace?"

"Yes. That's what he told me his name was."

The seaman pointed to a group of men who were now making their way up the gangplank carrying a single coffin. "Sir, that's Mr. Horrace."

Shaunessy looked at the men carrying the coffin and then back at the two ship employees. "I don't know what you mean. The man I met is on the ship, now. He is sitting next to me. We were having a conversation. It was only a few moments ago. We can board and see him ourselves."

The Captain waved the men with the coffin on and they continued to carry it aboard.

"Sir, Mr. Horrace is in that coffin. He died three days ago."

"But the man you described who had my luggage taken off the ship…you described him. You saw him."

"I didn't see him."

"I saw him, sir."

Shaunessy looked at the seaman. "Was the man who told you to remove my luggage from the ship Mr. Horrace or not?" Shaunessy asked.

"No. It couldn't have been."

Shaunessy dashed to the men carrying the coffin. "Wait!"

The four men stopped. The two ship employees joined them and Shaunessy looked to them. "Please. Have them open it."

The Captain looked at him.

"Sir, we can't do that," one of the seamen said.

The Captain turned to the coffin bearers. "Men, take it back down, set it down on the ground, and open it up for the gentleman."

The four men reluctantly walked back down the gangplank to do so.

"Here," the Captain said, handing one of them a small crowbar.

The man pried open one corner and repeated his action all around the coffin. The men opened the coffin.

Inside was the embalmed corpse of Mr. Horrace — the same man he was conversing with moments ago. He was even in the same clothes!

The men could see Shaunessy's face turn white.

"Is this the man you say was just speaking with you on the ship?" the Captain asked.

Shaunessy didn't answer him. He swallowed hard and just stared at the corpse.

"Men, close it up and get it on the ship," the Captain directed.

"Who was he?" Shaunessy asked. "What ... What did he do for a living?"

"You never heard of Mr. Horrace?"

Shaunessy stared at the coffin as the men lifted it up. "No, I never heard of him."

"He's from one the wealthiest families in Europe. I know him personally because I had the honor to work for him. My first job as a young man twenty years ago, and it was his kind reference that helped me obtain this job," the Captain answered. "Seeing that he's dead, sir, it concerns me that you claim you were sitting and talking to him."

"It was him. I'm not crazy or lying." He finally looked up at the seaman. "The person claiming to be my man—"

The other man was as pale as Shaunessy. The Captain noticed too.

"What's wrong?" the Captain asked. "You're not telling me you saw a dead man, too?"

"He wasn't dead. He was standing next to me and talking to me as you are now."

The Captain looked at both of them. "Is this some kind of prank by both of you?"

"Sir, how long have you known me?" the seaman asked.

"Why would I make up such a story?" Shaunessy asked the captain.

"You both are saying that you saw a dead man walking around. I have no time for games. Mr. Shaunessy, do you want your luggage on this ship or are you waiting for the next one?"

Shaunessy paused for a few moments to compose himself. "I'll wait for the next one."

"A few moments ago you were angry and demanded to be on this one. I will notify my colleagues about you, Mr. Shaunessy. We don't appreciate childish games."

"I'm not playing games."

"And you're in trouble too," the captain said to his crewman.

"Sir, why? I wouldn't make up such a thing."

"Go back to work. Good day, Mr. Shaunessy," he said in an annoyed tone.

Shaunessy stood next to his luggage for more than an hour, alone. He watched the *Indomitable* sail off. He couldn't go on the ship after this strange event. He wanted nothing to do with the ship, even if his trip to America would be delayed by weeks or even months.

The following month, Shaunessy heard the news. He was having his lunch at the local tavern.

The Indomitable had sunk off the coast of Bermuda, with all passengers and crew lost.

Martling

"There were ten of them. He was the ninth man."

His father, Doffue Martling, had lived in Sleepy Hollow for more years than even Old Man Van Tassel. His mother had passed some years back, and now his father took his turn to join her. His grave was next to hers, as it had always been planned, and young Isaiah Martling didn't take his gaze from their tombstones as the Pastor concluded a respectful prayer. It was 1798 and young Martling, at the age of twenty-two, found himself without any kin.

From the time of its founding, Sleepy Hollow—the Hollow to its reclusive residents, was such a small, tight-knit community, that anyone who died always got the respects of the whole town, and everyone attended. Doffue Martling's funeral was no different. Everyone of note in the town was there for the proceeding, from Old Man Van Tassel, Brom and Katrina Van Brunt, Mr. De Graaf and all the town elders, Mr. Berg, the caretaker, the Van Boors, the Mulders, Dutch and his men—all in the employ of Mr. Van Brunt—Mr. Tennant, the town doctor,

Hans Van Ripper, and Ms. Hancock, the teacher who instructed all the Hollow children in Tarry Town. Everyone wore their best Sunday attire in black.

Martling was a brawny, baby-faced young man with dark-brown hair. He had known everyone from the time he was a child and felt comforted by their attendance. True friends will be there when you most need them. This was young Martling's time of need; this small, but dignified affair. Somehow he managed to hold in his tears. The pastor adjourned the proceeding and slowly made his way to the young man.

"Thank you, pastor," Martling said as he shook the clergyman's hand.

"No need for sadness. He's with your mother. They are in a higher and better place, and both your folks are looking down with a deep sense of pride at the fine, young man they raised."

"Thank you, pastor." He felt the tears coming but held them back. "I'll always live to make them proud."

"Call on me anytime, if you need anything at all or don't need anything but want company or to talk. And it doesn't have to be a Sunday or in church, whenever you need anything."

"Yes, pastor. Thank you."

Katrina Van Brunt and some of the other townswomen began to gather around Martling. They gave him hugs and condolences.

"Isaiah Martling, please, my husband and father would like to have you come to our home for dinner," Mrs. Van Brunt said. "But when you're ready."

"Thank you, Mrs. Van Brunt."

He glimpsed Mr. Van Brunt and Old Man Van Tassel

watching from a few yards away.

"What will you do now?" Mrs. Mulder asked.

"Settle all my father's affairs, take charge of the property, and see about the will."

"If you need any help with moving things and such, come on by, and I'll get my lazy husband out there for you."

"Yes, that would be appreciated."

"There is no need for you to be alone at this time," said Mrs. Van Boor. "We'd also be happy to have you over for a good dinner."

Martling managed a smile. "Thank you. I will do that, for all of you."

"And don't wait too long."

"Yes, since I can't cook much more than some coffee that would be nice."

Some of the men walked to him and gave him their condolences as they collected their wives. The pastor offered to accompany him to Tarry Town, but he declined. He needed the time to himself.

Tarry Town was only two miles away. The day was overcast, though it was nearly noon. In this land and this time of the season, it was rarely fully bright. The sun did come to these parts, but it seemed some days as only an afterthought. No wonder there were so many haunted stories about the area. The Hollow was made for it.

Walking about in the Hollow, especially at night and alone, was what people avoided. The Horseman may have disappeared nearly eight years ago, freeing the people from his nightly rides of horror, but no one felt it would last. Some said the Horseman would return after three years, and when that passed, seven years. Now the conventional wisdom was that the chief apparition of the Hollow would return after thirteen years, if not before. In the meantime, there were plenty of other resident apparitions to maintain the town's haunted reputation. But for young Martling, it was a nice walk—a time to reflect.

It was the only thing that he and his father differed on. His father firmly believed in the Legend of the Headless Horseman and said he even saw it a few times with his own eyes. His father, though, was quite the terror himself—ornery, fearless, and wild in the face of any enemy, which the Redcoats found out the hard way during the Revolutionary War. The old, blue-haired man set out to take on a whole British platoon with his own nine-pounder cannon. He beat them back and saved the town single-handedly. That's what everyone told him.

Young Martling gave himself a good chuckle remembering those events. All of it important and larger-than-life at the time, as was his father; now part of history, mere memories. *What now?* He was now the last Martling left alive. His father came from an extremely large family, but according to his late parents' accounts, all of them were killed in some European battle—with honor, of course, or died from some ailment or disease. The burden fell to him to ensure the Martling name carried on. But the future at this moment, as his feet drew him closer to Tarry Town, was uncertain. His mother did the planning for him, then his father. He had no gift for self-direction, and no ability for making up the plans himself. He stopped in the middle of the road for a moment. He would have to plan his own life all by himself for the first time in his entire life. A chill ran done his spine. Forget ghosts and goblins; life is scary!

"It comes as no surprise," Mr. De Graaf said to Martling.

They sat in his small office as he leafed through the stack of documents on his desk.

"Your father had no debts and, as the sole heir, everything transfers to you. Please sign. Right here."

Young Martling leaned forward in his chair and took the ink pen from him to sign the documents as directed.

"What do you plan to do? It's a lot of land."

"I have to give it more thought."

"Give it all the thought you need. The only timetable is your own. I only ask, because I know you had spoken of going to Philadelphia or Boston or other parts."

"This is my home. I don't think I will be leaving for anywhere for some time. Until I decide on my plans. What do you think I should do?"

"It is a lot of land. You could sell it and get something more manageable, or even parts of it. Hasn't Mr. Van Brunt wanted to buy it from your father for years?"

"Yes, but I could never do that. My father was set on keeping the land in the family."

"As of today, you are the owner."

"I wish I knew what to do."

"My advice is to sell to Van Brunt. If not him, then you'd have to sell to an outsider. It's going to happen someday, but you don't want to be known as the one who broke tradition and let outsiders into the Hollow. And it's too much land for one young man to manage."

"I'll give it more thought."

"You could become an employer like Mr. Van Brunt. Hire your own men to work the land for you. You could make a handsome profit with a variety of crops."

"Me, an employer?"

"Yes, why not?"

"I'm not old enough to do that."

"How old do you have to be to order another man around? You have the land, and Mr. Boer would gladly give you a loan for expenses."

Martling leaned back in his chair and held the sides of his temple. De Graaf could see that the boy was becoming distressed.

"Go home and think about it. No decisions have to be made this instant, or even for a long time."

"I have too much to think about. That's the problem. I'm not good at any of this. Tell me what to do and where to go, and I can do that, but…"

"Don't think a second more about it. Today was the funeral. You're still grieving. Today is no day for talk of business. The land and everything on it is yours. You decide things when you decide them. In that, no one tells you what to do and where to go."

De Graaf stood from his chair, and Martling did the same.

"If you need any business or legal advice, I'm here. You know that."

"Yes, I'll be back when I'm ready." Martling's face flushed with distress again. "No."

"What is it?"

"My father's house, my house, is a complete mess. After mother passed, he never … he was never good at cleaning."

"Only making the mess."

"Yes."

It gave Martling a brief moment to smile as another fond memory came into his head.

"What about his old nine-pounder? Doffue Martling was not just your father and one of the town founders with Old Man Van Tassel. He was the collector of Hollow history. If I were you, I wouldn't start with going through his things in the house. I'd start with his workshop."

Martling perked up. "Yes, his workshop. The nine-pounder and all the weapons."

"He was quite the tinkerer and inventor, too. Wasn't he preparing for a full invasion by a new alliance of the British, French, and other no-goods against the Colonies—the States? He had quite the colorful vocabulary."

"He did, indeed," Martling said smiling. "He started making his own weapons from the time I was a child. The things he would say. He was constructing a cannon that could explode an entire British ship with one shot. Did he tell you that he was making a special musket that could hurt a ghost?"

"Harm a ghost?"

"He had so many ideas working in his workshop."

"What was he planning on doing, going after the Headless Horseman?"

De Graaf laughed and Martling touched his face. He was crying. De Graaf patted him on the back and walked him to the door.

"Go home and take all the time you need to relive those happy memories with him—both parents."

Martling nodded and took a handkerchief from his pocket to dry the tears from his face.

"The Martling Estate" was what the lawyer had said to him. A legal term and nothing more, he said. Martling sat on the front porch of the main house as the sun began to set. His father had built the house with his bare hands at least half a century ago. The structure was visibly old, but Doffue Martling built things to last, and it was likely that it would be standing half a century more. But as he gazed out across the fairly empty land, he saw nothing estate-like to any of it. It was old, and he was young. If he stayed here, he would be old too, long before his time.

He actually did the opposite of what Mr. De Graaf suggested. He began by sorting through his father's belongings in the house. It took much longer than it should have because he kept bursting out in tears or was fighting off another outburst. He wasn't ashamed to cry, but felt it had gone beyond normal emotional expressions of grief and loss. His whole body was a wreck. His muscles hurt, his face hurt, and even his teeth and eyeballs hurt. He never had issues with lack of energy, but he felt wasted. He sat on the porch, his back propped up against the house, staring off across his land. He sat for hours, and now it was almost dark.

Martling held his breath and, with all his might, stumbled to his feet. He exhaled loudly and walked down the steps and around the front of the house to the side. The thought of his father's workshop helped lighten his mood. Images of his father's many muskets and pistols, a real battle-tested cannon, and all his unique weapon inventions, filled his mind.

There probably was a fortune in weapons in the combination barn, weapons storage, and workshop, but the door was never locked. The Hollow was like every other tight-knit community in America. For most, not even the fear of wild Indians or creatures of the night could change their daily habits. Doffue Martling was a self-described, modern-day warrior but, as with everyone else, saw no need to take any precautions to secure his property and belongings in the town of his friends. The word thievery might as well not exist in enclave communities such as this.

He entered the main entrance of the barn and immediately began lighting the lanterns. He hung a few from hooks on the wall, another he placed on a large table, and another he rested on the ground. Martling then immersed himself in his late father's weapon collection; pistols and muskets of all makes and models—some going back to the late fourteenth century. He admired their craftsmanship, but he knew each one had a unique story, both in terms of its individual pedigree and how it came to be in his father's collection. It was another reason to lament the passing of his father. He would have given anything to hear another story about the weapons or anything else he cared to speak about.

There were also endless swords and daggers in the collection but, in this case, he had little fascination with cutting weapons. In many ways, he feared them more than a bullet from any musket or pistol. The thought of being cut apart, or skewered like a pig on a spit, made him ill.

The next hour he spent admiring his father's famed nine-pounder that he used against the British in the War. It was very ordinary, but knowledge of its extraordinary place in Sleepy Hollow history made it impressive, nonetheless.

Three hours inside the barn and he realized that he had surveyed nothing more than the one corner housing the collection. In fact, he realized that his father never showed him any other part of the barn, and it was a big barn. He glanced at the door and saw that it was the dark of night. None of his other chores were started and there were many that had to be done. He hated chores, but he always did them. There was no one left to scold him if he didn't, or was there? He looked up as if the roof of the barn was not there. He had to act as if his father and mother were still watching down on him, and he had to always make them proud.

THE HORSEMAN KILLER.

He saw the words immediately when he lifted the one lamp from the ground as he began to leave the barn.

The Horseman Killer?

His father called himself an inventor, but he was nothing more than a tinkerer, putting together odds and ends to create something new. What could he have possible created that he would give such a provocative name?

Martling approached the long crate nestled under the big table in a corner. He leaned down and grabbed it with one hand, dragging it out as he held the lantern with his other hand. He set the lantern down on the ground and undid the latch of the box. He lifted the lantern again and saw that what was inside the box was the length of a Brown Betty, but it wasn't a musket. It was a type of cannon—a cannon that a man could carry and shoot. Martling smiled.

He knew he was too old to behave the way he was, but he brandished the new weapon and pretended to be fending off single attackers, groups of ruffians, or a whole Red Coat army. He enacted the recoil of the weapon, though he had no idea what the recoil was, threw himself on the ground pretending to dodge counter-fire, and leapt up, mimicking the sounds of cannon fire with his mouth. The young Martling was working up quite the perspiration from all his horseplay.

He was tired and collapsed to the ground, cradling the Horseman Killer.

"Chores!" he yelled to himself.

He placed the weapon on the ground next to him as if it were a delicate instrument and grudgingly got to his feet, grabbing the lantern.

"That's one good thing about being dead, Pa! No more chores!"

With his lantern lighting the way, he left the barn and made his way back to the main house.

While he conducted himself as the new master of the Doffue Martling estate, he thought of nothing else but the weapon. He loved the sound a good musket made and couldn't contain his anticipation to fire his father's hand-cannon for the first time. He had already decided on the target. Perhaps he could blast the gnarly tree apart at the far end of the property with one shot. He smiled.

It was late in the night. He needed to be in bed as it was going to be another long day tomorrow but—*I want to shoot the hand-cannon*, he said to himself.

Martling marched out of the house, and then had to stop and double-back to grab the lantern. He made his way back to the barn, grinning like a toddler, with a spring in his step. It was the first time in a long time he was happy. He looked up to the sky and imagined his father was looking down at him smiling too and encouraging him to shoot the weapon as any man would want to.

He swung the door open. "Behold my Horseman

Killer!" he declared. "Let's go blast a tree to kingdom come."

Cough!

Martling spun around and stared out into the night with his arm extended forward with the lantern. His entire body was gripped with fear. *That cough. That was mother's cough!*

It was years, many years since he had heard it. It was something his mother always did. She never yelled, never raised her voice, and never lifted a hand in anger. What she would do is clear her throat with a cough. That's when you knew you were in trouble. She did it to him. She did it to his father. It would stop you in your tracks, because if you didn't set yourself on the right path, then the diminutive, seemingly meek woman would unleash her inner demon. She was every bit capable of becoming a Scottish terror as her husband. He unleashed against Red Coats. She unleashed against her 'lazy husband' and 'misbehaving son.'

But how can I hear a cough?

Martling stared out into the night, paralyzed. He closed his eyes for a moment, and then slapped himself.

"There is no such thing as ghosts."

He put it out of his mind and returned to what he had set out to do. The joy was gone, but he ignored the uneasy fear that replaced it. He was going to shoot his father's hand-cannon. That's what he set out to do, and that was what he was going to do.

Martling froze again.

As he stared into the barn through the open barn door, his eyes fixed on the hand-cannon lying on the ground. He didn't move; he didn't blink. This was becoming a very black night indeed, the kind of night given to haunted and unholy stories told to frighten little children—and grown adults. The weapon had moved! Or … something about it moved.

And it was how it moved.

Martling stepped closer. He threw the lantern at it.

The lantern smashed upon the hand-cannon, and the giant black snake coiled around it barely reacted. The sparse bits of hay on the ground began to catch fire, but the reptile seemed possessed to do nothing more than remain in place and…stare back at Martling.

The flames of burning hay were slowly going out, and the barn would return to pitch black. Martling still did not move and casually pushed his hands into his pockets. As the illumination began to dim, the snake's head slowly began to rise.

He had only been alive in this world for twenty-two years and didn't have the benefit of his father's knowledge, but he had never seen a snake like it before. He was positive no one had ever seen a snake like it in these parts, including his late father. He was positive no such snake species existed in America.

Martling saw in his mind's eye the future that would have been. A neighbor happening by the next day and finding his long-dead body sprawled upon the ground. The doctor would see the snake bite. Maybe the symptoms would appear as from a normal snake, even though the snake before him was far from normal. He knew so much about snakes because they were the only animals in the world that truly frightened him. Everything about them made his flesh crawl. He made sure to learn every fact about them so as to stay as far away from them as humanly possible. This snake was not normal. It never even flinched from the fire — very 'unsnake-like' behavior, he thought. The snake had but one purpose: to kill the bearer of the Horseman Killer.

But that was the future that would have been. His mother warned him with a simple cough. There was no other explanation. It could well be his imagination spurred on by his highly emotionally state. It probably was the wind or some stray animal, and his mind made him hear what he wanted to hear — needed to hear. The sound of a beloved, departed parent. Or, as the pastor would say, the forces of good and evil were battling all around them, and he was able to perceive it for only the tiniest fraction of an instant.

If what happened didn't happen, he would have marched into the barn, touched the hand-cannon, and been instantly killed. But that future was not to be. His mother warned him. The fire was breathing its last life. Martling pulled a handful of gunpowder from his pocket and tossed it. The flash of light blinded him as the explosion ripped through the air.

Martling ran to the table and quickly struck a match to light another lantern. He immediately looked down around his feet, and saw the snake blown apart. But in his mind, during the brief darkness, it had slithered to his feet. He walked forward with the lantern. The hand-cannon was untouched; the snake was scattered across the ground in pieces. He kicked the weapon.

"*Oww!*" Martling's head violently jerked as he yelled out.

He jumped back and looked at his boot. The snake's disembodied head was clamped down hard on his right boot.

"You evil snake!"

He hopped to one of the tables and grabbed a knife. He squeezed the handle with his face enraged, and slammed the blade into the snake's head.

What did I do?

His face turned pale-white. He had stabbed the snake through its disembodied head. But he also impaled his own foot. Martling's eyes fluttered as he collapsed to the ground.

Part III
The Patch

Julian Crane

"It haunts me nightly in my dreams — these hellish nightmares."

"Bad situations often come in threes. Not sure why," his father had said to him once.

Brom Bones. The murderous Marshal Damian. The Horseman.

His entire life, every significant memory—and every trivial one, and every stray thought—was engulfed and violently replaced with a singular entity that he had never encountered before and was wholly unprepared for—fear.

Caleb Williams was gripped with a terrified hysteria as it sprinted faster than its legs had ever done before. Julian hung onto him with all his might until somehow the reins broke. Then he frantically wrapped his arms around his horse's neck to stay on. The crushing fear had turned Julian's face pale as he fought the impulse to look back. He mustn't, he kept repeating to himself—yelling to himself. If he looked back, it would get him. But he was losing the battle not to do so.

They reached it! They were upon the bridge and about to cross. He relented and looked back. The pumpkin projectile filled his entire view as it came hurtling at his face. He jerked his head to the side, but the impact smacked his jawbone, threw him from the horse, and smashed him into the bridge with a deafening impact.

A terrified Caleb Williams continued across, picking up speed rather than slowing for his master. Julian, empowered by sheer adrenaline alone, rose up and ran across the bridge too, oblivious to his pain or injuries—he was running for his life. Julian made it across and followed the dust trail left behind by his fleeing horse. He glimpsed back across the river as he sprinted over the hills.

Through a haunting mist, the Headless Horseman sat on its black horse of death. And every pumpkin on its islet domain was glowing.

He remembered nothing more of his brush with the Horseman and its ever-present companion—Death.

Hans Van Ripper rode his wagon into Tarry Town for his weekly supply run. He worked in the livery stables three times a week and planned to continue to do so until he was physically unable, or until he just up and died of old age.

He noticed something was amiss as soon as he passed the main inn. Feverish talk, in loud anxious voices, came from a group of men gathered to the side of the street. They became interested in him as soon as they saw him. One of the men gestured to someone across the street.

Hans turned his head and a man he had never seen before, wearing a large cowboy hat and rifle dangling from his hand, began to approach.

"Good morning, mister," he said. "Are you Hans Van Ripper?"

Hans stopped his one-horse driven wagon. "I am. Who are you?"

"I was about to ride out to your place. I'm Marshal Wilcox."

"Another marshal," Van Ripper said in his usual irritable way. "How many marshals are going to come through this way?"

"I should be the only one for a while. I'll most likely be appointed to cover this region. Hopefully, people will come to know and rely on me. Do you know a Marshal Julian Crane?"

"Yes, I do, but you already know that. Why? What's happened?"

"Papa, I can feed myself," the little boy said with playful indignation.

Brom Bones laughed. "Yes, you are a big boy." He handed the fork back to the boy.

Brom Bones sat at the head of the dining room table, close to his son in the adjacent chair whose head barely reached above the table. Katrina Van Brunt returned to the table and sat on the other side.

The boy was always restless and began to tell his parents all the things he was going to do for the day while he wolfed down his food.

"I don't think the day is long enough to do all that," Brom challenged, jokingly.

"Yes, I can, Papa."

Old Man Van Tassel entered the room with a different 'favorite' pipe and walked over to his grandson, smiling. "You've finished your meal so fast already."

"Yes, Grandpa. Last week was my birthday so I'm a big boy now."

"I see that. Go outside and play while I talk to your folks."

The boy jumped up from the table and dashed to the front door. Katrina knew it was pointless to try to tell him to slow down in the mansion.

"I thought I should tell you both." Van Tassel's expression changed from jovial to serious. "Julian Crane is back in Sleepy Hollow."

The smiles disappeared from Brom and Katrina's faces.

"Why?" Katrina asked furiously. "To try to harm this family again? We're ready for him this time."

Van Tassel took his pipe from his mouth and gestured with the same hand for calm. "Mr. Julian Crane was carried into town by a lawman. Apparently, Marshal Damian is dead."

"Dead? How?" Brom asked.

"Did this Julian Crane kill him?" Katrina asked.

"This Julian Crane," Van Tassel continued, "is under the town doctor's care for a condition related to fear, panic, and shock. They say he escaped the Horseman."

The Van Brunts went pale.

Julian lay in the barn staring up at the roof. At least here there was no sickening quiet. He could hear chirping crickets, sometimes birds, and from time-to-time the same owl that staked out the area as its own. Van Ripper had turned the section of the barn into sleeping quarters for him with a firm cot, thick blanket, and a few small pillows. The barn door opened, and Van Ripper entered.

"You're going to have to start paying me for lodging," he said.

Julian looked at him without moving his head. "No arguments from me," he answered softly.

"The doctors said you won't get up from the bed. You've been lying there for more than a week. What's wrong with you?"

"I want to have one good night of sleep. I can't seem to get at ease."

"You need to snap out of this and go about your life. You found what you were looking for. Go home now. Hiding in bed, or in my barn, isn't going to solve anything."

"I haven't found what I'm looking for."

"What do you mean? You have. I told you what happened to your uncle, Ichabod, the very first day you came to Sleepy Hollow, but you were too city-sophisticated and bull-headed to believe me. Now you know what I said was true; what everyone in the Hollow knows. The Horseman took your uncle from this world, claiming his soul in the dark of night, like so many others before him, on its devilish quest for its head. You know it too. Go home."

Julian sat up slowly in the cot. "My mission hasn't changed. I'm going to hunt it, and then I'll go home."

Hans smirked, but then his orneriness returned. "The Horseman killed your uncle. There's nothing else to do."

"There is."

"No, there isn't. You saw the hellish thing with your

own two eyes, and look at the state it put you in. You go near it again and no one will ever see you again. Just like Ichabod."

"You're right. If I were to go there alone. But I won't be going there alone. And I don't mean my horse and my gun."

"What do you mean? No fool will ride with you to hunt the Horseman. Hunt? What does that even mean? Hunt? You can't hunt a spirit of evil."

"The Indians had braves who hunted unearthly things of evil like ghosts and witches."

Hans laughed. "We first met and you were of the firm opinion that those who believed in the supernatural were the worst kind of fools. Now you've turned into your late uncle, believing all kind of ghost stories. Are you an Indian ghost-hunter, or witch-hunter, or a lawman? You ain't even Indian."

"I didn't believe in the evil supernatural. That was until the Horseman was chasing after me to drag me to Hell, as close to me as you are now."

"Then go home. It's better to tell haunted stories to your children and grandchildren than to be the unfortunate victim of one of those stories."

"Mr. Van Ripper." Julian had transformed before his very eyes from the frail, pitiful man that was brought to his barn, near death from fear, to the Julian he knew — unwavering, bull-headed determination, even — no — especially, in the face of overwhelming odds. "I will not stop until I hunt down the foul murderer of my uncle Ichabod. I'll either do it, or I'll die trying."

"Then Julian, you'll be joining your dear uncle in the after-life."

Julian lay back down on the cot. "Lots of enemies have underestimated me. Brom, Marshal Damian, but I'm still here."

"Those were men. This is the Horseman. The two are not even remotely the same. Wait a moment. Marshal Damian?" Hans changed his tone. "We found out something about him after you left with him."

"That he was a sick, evil murderer," Julian said with anger.

"What? You knew?"

"He was an agent of the Horseman."

"Agent? What do you mean?"

"At least he did something good in his evil life."

"You killed him?"

"He led me to the new lair of the Headless Horseman," Julian said ignoring him.

"What? How? Where?" Hans face was flushed; his mind racing.

"Yes, I killed him. Too bad I couldn't have done it sooner. No telling how many innocent people he did away with."

"You know where the Horseman lives? The Horseman hasn't been seen in the Hollow for a decade. Everyone thinks the Horseman has returned to the Hollow and chased you."

"No, it has a new home-base. I was there. A cursed patch of an island far from any human civilization, but surrounded by black storm clouds and rabid animal sentinels. I know where it lives now. It should have killed me. It's going to regret that. It's going to regret killing my uncle Ichabod, because no normal man was his nephew. I am his nephew."

Hans had a look of fear on his face. Not from the thought of the return of the Horseman, but the change in Julian's outward appearance again. If any mortal man could vanquish the Headless Horseman, it was indeed Julian Crane.

Total Fear

"I'm coming for you, Horseman. My name is Vengeance."

Ahhh! Mrs. Bakker sat erect in her bed, awoken by her nightmare in a cold sweat. Her scream also woke her giant of a husband in the adjacent twin bed.

In the early morning of the next day, outside the general store, they stood before the crowd. The tiny woman was dressed in black, her head covered by a dark shawl. Her giant of a husband stood quietly behind her in his black clothes. He never wore a hat on his balding head.

The crowd listened to them with fear.

"I warned everyone, didn't I?" she said. "I said this man, this Julian Crane man, would bring Hell back to the Hollow. We were free of its evil for ten years. None of us mentioned its name and we were free of it, but this Crane man trespassed into Tarry Town, into the Hollow. His very words have resurrected the Horseman.

"Which one of us" —her voice rose as she pointed at the crowd, with tiny fingers on her miniature hand, moving side-to-side—"will become the Horseman's next victim?

"

Which one among us will be snatched from this world, from our families, out of the darkness of night? Which one us will be taken to Hell?"

The look of sheer terror showed on every man and woman's face that listened to her.

"We have brought this on ourselves. We should have dealt with this Crane man as soon as we knew who he was, and what he was—a harbinger of death. That's what he is! He has brought the Horseman back to the Hollow, and for that … he must be killed."

Gasps came from the crowd.

Three of the elders burst into the office of Mr. De Graaf, startling both he and his client, a townsman reviewing a prepared legal document.

"De Graaf, you have to follow us this instant!" Mr. Boer cried.

"What's happening?"

"The entire town is marching to Van Ripper's place," Mr. De Wit answered.

"They're going after Julian Crane," Mr. Boer said. "They mean to kill him for bringing the Horseman back to the Hollow."

Mrs. Bakker and her husband led the nearly sixty-person crowd of men, women, and even a few children down the dirt road from Tarry Town to Sleepy Hollow. No one spoke as they marched to Van Ripper's place. As they came over the ridge, they could see Hans Van Ripper standing on his porch with his wood-chopping ax in his hand.

"What you doing on my land?" he yelled out.

"Where's that Julian Crane man?" one of the men asked.

"Why? He's a guest. You're not. Get off my land."

"Hans, there's a whole lot of us and only one of you," another man said.

"Old man, get inside your cabin and send Crane out. He has to answer for some things," a younger man directed. "This doesn't concern you."

"You're on my land so it concerns me. I'll say it again. Get off my land before I get my rifle and start shooting me some full-grown trespassers."

A man ran around to the front of the crowd from behind. It was Dr. Tennant with a look of distress on his face.

"What are you doing?" he asked.

"Doctor, this is none of your concern. This is between the town and Julian Crane," Mrs. Bakker said to him.

"Julian Crane is in my care. The man barely survived an encounter with the Horseman. You all know that. What are you preparing to do?"

"Doctor, we are making sure that we don't have an encounter with the Horseman. If he's not here, maybe the Horseman will leave us be again. We'll do anything to prevent its return, even if that means killin'."

Tennant was shocked and looked into the faces of the crowd. All were of the same mind.

"I understand your fear. I truly do. I don't want it back any more than anyone else, but what gave you the notion that the Horseman returned because of him?"

"Doctor, it disappeared after it took Ichabod and returns when his nephew comes to town. No. He has to go now. Alive, or dead, if it's necessary."

"I've never seen such a bunch of fools," Hans yelled. "Returned? The Horseman hasn't returned to the Hollow."

"It has," Mrs. Bakker said.

"Says who? Have you seen it?"

"In nightmares that shake me to a screaming fear every single night."

"Hmm. That's a no then."

Mrs. Bakker's husband huffed in anger and started towards Van Ripper.

"Your husband takes one more step, and I'll cut him as if he's a block of wood." Hans gripped the handle of his ax.

"No," Tennant yelled as he stepped between the men with his arms extended.

"You all don't know anything," Hans said. "The Horseman isn't back."

"Yes, it is," a man yelled back. "It killed Marshal Damian and almost killed the Julian Crane man. He's trouble. He's been trouble since he set foot in this valley. He's the cause of it."

"The Horseman didn't kill Marshal Damian."

"Then who did?"

"I did."

Julian Crane stood at the open doorway of Hans Van Ripper's cabin with a pistol in his hand.

The crowd watched him closely. They all recalled what he did to Brom Bones' gang and to Brom Bones himself.

"The best way for a lawman to control an unruly crowd is to identify its ringleaders." Julian's eyes locked on the Bakkers. "You deal with them forcibly, violently if you have to, and the rest loses all aggression and goes docile."

Mrs. Bakker glanced at her husband for a second. They looked at each other and then back at Julian.

"There is no need for any violence," Tennant said to Julian, and then repeated the same thing to the crowd.

"Firstly, the Horseman is not back. I didn't encounter it here. I encountered it far from here. It's new hellish home away from Hell. That's where I was, and that's where it tried to kill me."

The crowd looked at each other.

"Secondly, I killed Marshal Damian because he was an agent of the Horseman."

Sounds of disbelief came from the crowd.

"He must have killed many men in cold-blood in service to the Horseman. He tried to with me, and I buried a tomahawk in his skull and watched a pack of wolves drag his body away into oblivion."

Mothers covered the ears of their children.

"Thirdly, I'm going back to the Horseman's new home."

A look of shock came across everyone's face—except for Hans who stood quietly.

"I told you all that I was going to hunt down the foul murderer of my dear Uncle Ichabod. It wasn't Brom Bones. It wasn't Marshal Damian. I can admit when I was wrong. You all told me who it was, what it was. Now, I know it to be true, so that's where I'm going. I'm going back to the Horseman's home to destroy it any way I can. I don't know how, but I will. It's going to regret it let me escape. And anyone here—man or woman—that attempts to stop me is going to regret being born. In fact, I'm going to start counting to ten, and if any of you are still standing in front of Mr. Van Ripper's place, and not running back the way you came, in quick fashion, *I'm* going to come to your house and snatch you up in the middle night, bundle you up, and deliver you, personally, into the skeleton arms of the Horseman."

Hans had to forcibly grip his mouth with both hands to muffle his laughter from the human dust cloud. He had never seen people run away so fast.

Help Wanted

"Kill it! Kill it anyway you can!"

"Go away, Julian Crane."

It was the unsaid words on the face of every man and woman who he came across.

Julian Crane rode into Tarry Town. Hans Van Ripper had asked his current intentions yesterday, but he didn't answer. He had only worked it out in his own head as he lay down to sleep the previous night.

"If you know the Horseman killed your uncle, and it was not Brom Bones, why are you still here?" Mr. Berg, the undertaker, asked him as he passed. "Don't you have somebody waiting for you back home? Shouldn't you be going back there?"

Berg's disposition was probably no different than anyone else he'd meet all day.

The busiest place in all of Tarry Town was the main tavern near the front of town. Within eyeshot were the general store, the inn, the new school, the livery stables, the bank, and the church. Julian rode up, tied up his horse, and walked inside.

Moments later, Julian walked back out with a chair and placed it in front of the porch to the side. He walked back inside. Moments later, he came out with a big sign and some tools to hammer it to one of the building's support poles for the overhead wooden awning. He went back inside.

Townspeople had already begun to gather and gossip. No one in the streets could believe what they were reading on the sign. Julian came out of the tavern, walked down the steps, and took his seat in the chair on the ground. Men came out of the tavern to look at the sign, people emptied shops, and people rode up on horses. They read the sign in disbelief.

HELP WANTED! JOIN U.S. MARSHAL'S POSSE TO HUNT DOWN THE FOUL MURDERER OF ICHABOD CRANE. GENEROUS COMPENSATION. ALL BONAFIDE INQUIRIES WELCOME.

"Mister?" a man asked from his horse. Julian looked up at him. "Ichabod Crane was killed by the Horseman."

"I know."

A look of shock came across the man and he rode off as fast as he could.

"You're putting together a posse to hunt down the Headless Horseman?" a man from the tavern asked incredulously.

"Yes. Hunt it down and destroy it," Julian said with conviction and hate.

The entire crowd of people stared at him, looking for any sign of doubt or mischief in him. He was not joking. People moved away from him as quickly as they could. U.S. Marshal Julian Crane was mad!

The first day Julian sat in his chair there was a lot of

foot traffic around him. People would sometimes stand in the road, read the sign, look at him in disbelief, and read the sign again. This would sometimes go on for a quarter of an hour, a half hour, or more. People would ask him if it was a joke. Some would ask him if he was insane. Others asked if is he was allowed to do such crazy things as an agent of the government. One man asked if he suffered from a head wound from the War.

The second day, people just stayed away from him. They watched him from the opposite side of the street, from windows and door entrances. The murmur of their gossiping was sometimes so loud that not only could Julian hear their words, but he was sure someone sitting miles away could hear them too.

No one could believe that Julian was serious about this prospect. It was day four, and all he did was sit in his chair from sunup to sundown. He would take breaks to get food, use the outhouse, and feed and water his horse, but that was it. There was something almost supernatural about his own determination to sit in that chair and find men for his 'cursed suicide posse' as the town was now calling his mission.

On day six, the Elders came around and threatened to call the law on him. Julian didn't even answer them. He just sat there. The Elders, exacerbated, walked away back to their businesses.

On day seven, a town hall meeting was convened in Tarry Town on the Sabbath. It was the only day that Crane did not go into town for his mission. Something had to be done about the Julian Crane man. Businesses said he was scaring away customers. The schoolteachers said he was scaring the children, and parents said their children were having nightmares about the Horseman now. The pastor said that Crane's presence was not a godly thing and that it would certainly encourage the Horsemen to return to the Hollow. It was decided that Julian would have to be removed from his daily perch somehow—threaten him, pay him, anything.

It was the start of the second week. Julian sat on his chair quietly, as always. The Elders stood in front of the bank building with all the businessmen in Tarry Town. They watched him, collectively waiting to build up enough courage to confront him.

The streets were packed with people, watching and waiting for the final confrontation between the Elders and Crane. Even the normal school day was canceled and all the children—not shy like the rest of the townsfolk—sat right on the porch of the tavern behind Julian. They would have front-pew seats to the showdown.

Then Brom Bones rode into town on his famed horse, Daredevil. Brom was dressed in his best, as usual, and had his favorite tan brim hat. The Van Brunts always set the fashion for the region, and men had already begun buying the same hat. Katrina Van Brunt had the same effect on all the womenfolk.

Julian saw him when he first appeared around the corner, but he looked away and down to the ground. He would make no eye contact whatsoever with the man he once thought to be his uncle's killer—the man he almost shot in front of his little son. Brom made no acknowledgment of Julian either.

There were smiles on many faces in the crowd. Had Brom come to remove the miscreant himself? He had more cause to do so than anyone else. Even the Elders looked at each other, smiling. Brom had come to the rescue!

Brom dismounted his horse, walked past the seated Julian, up the steps to the sign, and pulled it down from the post. The children were all squirming around trying to see what he was going to do.

"You," Brom pointed at one boy. "Go get me a hammer and nails."

"Yes, Mr. Van Brunt." The boy disappeared inside the tavern.

Brom reached into his coat and took out a brush.

"Hold this can," Brom directed one of the girls.

Brom dipped the brush in the paint can and started to write something on the sign. He finished it, stared at it for a moment, and then nodded to himself. He handed the brush to the girl who stood on her tiptoes to see what he wrote. The boy was back, and Brom took the nails and hammer. He promptly hammered the sign back to the spot it was before on the post. He gave the hammer and nails back to the boy.

"Give the brush and paint to your teacher tomorrow," Brom said to the girl. "Your class can put it to use."

"Thanks, Mr. Van Brunt," the girl said, smiling.

Brom walked back down the steps to his horse. He jumped back on his Daredevil and rode off.

Julian sat there for a moment and sighed. *What did Brom do to my sign?* If he ruined it, Julian decided he would give up right there. He would not go against Brom. He'd leave Tarry Town and never come back. He'd give up his quest.

He looked up and noticed all the people in the street reading the sign with their mouths hanging wide-open. He looked near the bank and saw the Elders trying to get De Graaf back on his feet. *The man had fainted.* Julian turned around in his chair to read the sign.

~~HELP WANTED!~~ JOIN U.S. MARSHALL'S POSSE TO HUNT DOWN THE FOUL MURDERER OF ICHABOD CRANE. ~~GENEROUS COMPENSATION. ALL BONAFIDE INQUIRIES WELCOME.~~ $10,000 BOUNTY REWARD FOR EACH MAN!

The Gang

"No specter dares to show its face!"

Julian had suspicions about what the next days might bring. He arose from Van Ripper's barn around midnight with lantern in hand and rode back into Tarry Town. He had taken only a brief nap in his clothes. He arrived and roused the inn keeper who lived on the ground-level, and after listening to a tirade about the indecency of the hour, was still rented a room.

At sunrise, the main street in front of the main tavern was a menagerie of every type of human that walked the earth. All of them waiting for Julian, and the spectator line went far down the road and out of town. Everyone eager to see the nephew of the late and unfortunate Ichabod Crane gallop into town.

With everyone looking one way, Julian was able to stand in the back and survey the crowd. There were plenty of gunmen but many more 'wannabes.' There were men posing with their gun or rifle, a barrel-chested man holding an axe in each hand, and there was a lanky man juggling three rifles.

What threat did this juggler suppose he would be to the Horseman — make it laugh itself to death?

Julian walked into the tavern unseen by the crowd, strolled up to the counter, and the proprietor behind it almost choked on his drink. Julian tossed down a few coins.

"I need a small table for my chair and some writing paper."

"Yes, Mister Crane. I mean, Marshal Crane." The proprietor ran off to the back.

Julian exited the establishment, walked down the steps, dusted off his chair, and sat.

A woman glanced over and noticed him. She screamed out, "He's here!"

Julian watched the entire crowd on the street turn in unison to look at him. He couldn't help but to smile to himself. The proprietor came out of the tavern and jumped down the steps to place a small table in front of Julian, and then he pulled out a nicely bound journal from behind his waistband, and a pencil from behind his ear, placing both on the table.

"There you go, Marshal Crane."

"Thank you." Julian opened up the empty journal, put the pencil in the center of the pages, and closed the book. The proprietor watched him, smiling. Julian looked up again and saw that everyone was watching his every move.

Julian stood from his chair and raised his hand up high. "I want everyone to queue up behind this man here."

The man was more like a boy. He carried a rifle almost as long as he was tall. The boy allowed Julian to push him back a few spaces in front of the desk. Immediately, people began to line up behind him.

"What's your name, boy?"

"Benjamin, Mr. Crane."

"Do your folks know you're here?"

"Yes sir, Mr. Crane. My pa sent me. My ma said we'd be able to live like royalty like the Van Brunts with the kind of money you're giving out."

Julian smiled and then the smile was gone.

"What do you suppose this posse will be setting out to do?"

"Hunt down the Headless Horseman, Mr. Crane!" The boy smiled wide and people were laughing and cheering at his exclamation.

Julian gestured for the boy to draw closer. The boy did so, and Julian leaned forward. The boy leaned down. Julian whispered into his ear for a few moments. The boy jerked up, his expression turning to fear, he lifted up his rifle and ran away down the street.

Julian stood up and walked to the topmost step of the tavern to address the crowd. "There seems to be some confusion here, so I will explain fully so that there will be none. This is not a fox-hunt, bear-hunt, wolf-hunt, fowl-hunt, or fishing excursion. We are going to set out to kill the Headless Horseman of Sleepy Hollow, the most frightful thing to ever haunt these lands. We will have to travel a good long ways to get to it, and the lands we have to travel through are both inhospitable and deadly to mortal men.

"I saw the Horseman once, and I was running for dear life, and I am no coward. I'm a young man but, yes, my hair is turning white. All because of that one encounter with the Horseman. I ran so fast that I was basically bedridden for over a week. The doctor said I had used my legs at an exertion level that God had not designed them for. My horse used to be able to sleep through a cannon blast. Now, it's struck by nervousness, even if he hears a cricket.

"Mr. Van Brunt is a very generous and noble patron, indeed, to help set up this posse, but if you don't realize right now that you shall probably die a horrible and miserable death, like my poor uncle a decade ago, then you aren't merely a fool. You are dangerous and I don't want you. I am going to kill that foul murderer of my poor uncle, and I am only going to bring men with me worthy of this mission. If you are not a lawman, trained killer, or seasoned soldier, turn around and go home this instant."

Julian stepped down and returned to his chair.

People stood quietly and looked at him. The crowd gradually thinned out as people reluctantly turned and began to leave. An hour later, the streets were virtually empty. People, again, watched from the windows, doorways, porches, and from around corners. All that was left was a lonely Julian at his chair in front of the tavern.

His face was not worried. *Tomorrow the real candidates will be getting into town,* he said to himself.

It was just before dawn when Julian set out of Van Ripper's cabin to ride into Tarry Town. He led his horse by the reins to the barn door. As soon as he opened it, he saw someone was waiting.

"If this is about the posse, then you'll have to see me in town like everyone else," Julian muttered as he mounted Caleb Williams.

"I'm sorry, Mr. Crane. But I'm a Sleepy Hollow lad. I figured I'd ride in with you."

"Who are you?" Julian asked.

"My name's Isaiah Martling. Doffue Martling was my father and he was good friends with Mr. Van Ripper. He can vouch for me."

"If you say. I'm surely not going to bother Mr. Van Ripper about it now."

"I wouldn't want you to, but my father was a fearsome man in a fight. He took on an entire British attachment by himself when they tried to invade the Hollow."

"You're telling me this, why?"

"I want to join your posse. But I didn't want you to embarrass me in front of the whole town if you didn't want me. I live here, after all."

"Why should you be a part of my posse? Sounds like your father is the man I need, but I know he's passed."

Martling looked to be around eighteen with a fresh freckled face and uncombed, wild hair beneath a worn hat. But he was a brawny lad, made so from many a day of hard fieldwork. He looked like he could do some real physical damage to more than one man with his fists.

Then he lifted his weapon. Julian at first thought it was some of kind of log and then noticed it was made of metal with three separate rings of wood at about foot-long intervals.

"My late father made it," Martling said. "He made all kinds of new weapons to use against the British. He had his own nine-pounder cannon that could sink an entire battleship. He made this because he wanted something more powerful than any rifle in his hand—it can blow an entire British platoon to bits." Martling showed him a fist-sized metal ball. "This is the round it shoots. Imagine what it might do to a certain specter in question. He gave it a name too—the Horseman Killer."

Martling had Julian's full attention. "But if it's a ghost, bullets and projectiles would pass through it."

"But is it really a ghost, Mr. Crane? I've heard the legend all my life. Not one time did I ever hear about the Horseman passing through solid objects or flying through the air. Other than riding around without a head, and disappearing at convenient moments, all the accounts tell of a thing that can be touched and can touch you. Wouldn't you want someone on the posse with a cannon like mine when the Horseman came at us? At the very least, we could blast those devilish pumpkin missiles out of its evil hand."

Julian's body shivered at the mere mention of the projectiles that he had encountered.

"Mr. Martling, welcome to the Super Posse."

Tarry Town often had travelers from all over the new United States and abroad, but the ones today were different. Whether in fancy dress, normal attire, or dirty clothes, all of these men had one thing in common—they all asked where to the find the man hiring the ten-thousand-dollar-a-man posse.

"A headless what?" the first real gunman of the day asked incredulously.

"Headless Horseman," Julian answered. He figured he was going to have to explain himself many more times today, and to men who were as skeptical as he, the day he first rode into town.

"Now how can a headless horseman see to ride, let alone kill somebody? Is this some kind of town joke? If so, I expect to get compensated for my time and travel."

"It's no joke," Julian replied. "My uncle is dead, so it's no joke to me. If you don't want to be part of the posse, then no one is forcing you. I am the one who must approve every member before we ride out."

"Well I'm not going out to hunt no ghost." The man started to walk off. "I expect to be compensated."

Julian ignored the man as he walked away.

"Tell me about this bounty?" another man asked. The man was incredibly sun-tanned and finely dressed with a white brim hat. Two impressive pistols rested in his holsters. Julian noticed the multi-colored bead necklace around his neck.

"How much did you overhear of my talk to that other man?" Julian asked.

"All of it."

"And you're not opposed to hunting down an apparition?"

"Indians have known, seen, and hunted down supernatural beasts on these lands long before the White man arrived. My late father was the best tracker who ever lived. No man or beast could escape him, and he passed those secrets on to me as his father had done before him. He was also a witch hunter."

Julian studied him. "Who are you, mister?"

"My name is Chief Baltimore. Gun-for-hire."

"You a tracker?"

"I am."

"The posse could use a tracker."

"Where is the posse going?"

"North, just shy of the Canadian border."

Baltimore nodded and said, "Fine. Been in similar terrain."

"Do you need to know about the thing we're hunting?"

"Not necessary. The relevant matter is the men who will make up the posse. If it is made up of brave men, then they will march to their foolhardy deaths. If it is made up of foolish men, the posse will abandon the mission long before we ever get there. If it is made up of wise men, then you may have a small — very small — chance of returning."

"Well, I'm in the wise category."

"Or the foolish category. Perhaps you want to gather up more fools to go with you. I'll see for myself."

Julian smiled. "Perhaps."

"Who do you have on this posse so far?"

"You're looking at them."

Baltimore glanced at Martling. "A man-boy and a boy-boy."

Martling jumped up from the chair. "I'm no boy." He lifted his cannon-gun.

Baltimore nodded. "A boy-boy with a big gun." He looked back at Julian. "Not a very impressive start in my eyes. Not one of you ever encountered this apparition —"

"I did. And I came here to put together this posse."

"You did?" Baltimore was now interested.

Julian removed his hat. "I went there with black hair. I came back with gray hair."

Baltimore watched him for a moment before turning around and walking away down the dirt street.

Martling sat down. "Are we ever going to put this posse together?"

"It will come together when it comes together. We need the right people, not just people. I could go alone if I wanted that."

"Look," Martling said.

Baltimore came back riding a beautiful, brown mustang. He dismounted and walked it to the side of the tavern to tie up. They kept watching him as he walked around them, up the steps of the tavern, and proceeded to lie down on the bench against the wall, covering his face with his hat.

Julian and Martling looked at each other.

"Is it nap time already?" Julian asked, somewhat sarcastically.

"Let's see if you know the difference between brave, foolish, and wise men Mr. Marshal Julian Crane." Baltimore's voice came out from under his hat.

"We need brave gunmen on this, don't we?" Martling asked. "I'm brave, and I'm going."

Julian explained, "Brave and smart are not the same thing. That's what he means."

"Well, it still makes no sense to me." Martling turned and yelled at Baltimore, "And I'm no boy-boy. And what kind of name is Baltimore for an Indian? That's no Indian name. I figure your real Indian name is 'One-Who-Talks-With-a-Mouth-Full-of-Dung!'"

It started as a chuckle, and then Baltimore exploded into laughter. Martling couldn't help but to start laughing too, and so did Julian.

Baltimore sat up and looked at Martling. "That is my Indian name."

Martling and Julian laughed harder.

There was the massive overweight man whose belly peeked out from under his shirt. There was the gaunt, stick figure man, slimmer than even the late Ichabod Crane. There was the bearded one with the twitchy eye.

The rifle-juggler man returned, wearing no less than four pistols on his waist belt.

Julian wrote names in his book, but declined all of them for one reason or another. He needed a team of men, that in the end, would have to depend on one another for their very lives, and possibly, even their mortal souls. This would be a posse like no other. He needed a team of equals.

"Lord Hallen is the name." The man in the top hat was better dressed than Brom Van Brunt or Chief Baltimore. He had the most delicately coiffed beard and mustache. His boots were well-worn but didn't have a speck of dirt on them. Even his horse was groomed to perfection. "Am I before the proper gentleman to inquire about the now-famous bounty?"

"Yes, you are," Julian answered.

"How does one get to be a Lord?"

Julian and Martling turned. Baltimore was sitting up straight on his bench—a brief change from his perpetual nap—to join in the asking of questions.

"The honor and distinction of a royal title can only be bestowed upon noble British gentlemen of distinction," Lord Hallen answered.

"You're British?" Martling asked.

"I am indeed. A birthright I'm proud of."

"You might not want to say that too loud around these parts," Julian informed.

"Why shouldn't I? I have nothing to be ashamed of."

"What side did you take in the War?" Julian asked suspiciously.

"Neither, my fine man. I've been traveling back and forth between the colonies, now the United States, and

Great Britain for nearing twenty years. Why should I go to war against either one or join on the side of either one? I am a businessman. I did business with both before the War, and I continue to do business with both after the War. As a gentleman, I only make war against a man who has directly done me harm. Not by the proxy made by any King or President. But I have no quarrel against any man whose convictions moved his heart to fight for his own noble cause— American or British." Lord Hallen smiled.

"Tell me about yourself?" Julian asked.

Had Julian been able to glimpse into the future, he would never have asked the question. Julian thought to himself, how the Lord could talk. By now, the entire town seemed to be gathered around the man to hear his fanciful exploits of the world over in his rich, distinctly British, baritone voice. How he defeated Indians here, tribesmen there, and ruffians in one city or the next. Even Baltimore was mesmerized. Julian thought that the Chief might give up the whole posse hunt to join 'his royal highness.'

Unfortunately, not everyone who came to inquire was as entertaining. Most couldn't even put two words together. However, when the conversation came to particulars of the subject of the bounty—the Horseman— the Lord suddenly had 'other business to attend to.' He ducked into some establishment. Later in the day, one of the town lads came for his expensive horse.

The next day brought the more seasoned gunmen to town. These men were not overeager or desperate. They were good. They knew it and no longer had the inclination to prove it to anyone. Today the business was serious and Julian had both Martling and Baltimore sitting at the table with him. His interviewing was deliberate, and his note-taking was thorough. The background (as stated) of each man was impressive, and the interviews started at first light, went straight through noon, and didn't end until an hour after it got dark. Julian felt obligated to talk to every man. They had all come a long way and waited a long time.

Martling's smile could be seen in the dark. He and Julian rode out of town to Van Ripper's place. "We have your posse for sure, Mr. Crane. You can pick from the best of the best."

"I don't know if we can wait for the best of the best. That could be months from now. The news about the posse is still traveling. But I'll decide on the posse tomorrow."

"We're leaving tomorrow?"

"No. Day after. I want us to have a full day together as a group before we ride out. Everyone must know the plan."

"Plan, Mr. Crane?"

"Plan. We're not going to just ride up on the Horseman and say 'please drop dead, even though we know you're dead,' ride back and collect the bounty money."

Martling thought for a moment. "Why shouldn't we do it that way? I'll just blast it with my hand-cannon and that ends it."

"Believe me, Martling, it's going to bad, very bad, and far from that easy."

Julian had been up most of the night reviewing his notes. He wanted to pick the posse members before noon. Surprisingly, he wasn't tired as he and Martling rode back into town early in the morning.

"Are you Marshall Julian Crane?"

A group of horsemen was waiting for them a half-mile outside the town. Julian continued to be amazed by all the strangers who knew him by sight.

"I am, but I'm not going to do any business in the middle of the road."

"Then we'll follow," the lead man said.

It was only a bit after dawn, so they couldn't see the horsemen clearly without the full daylight. Julian and Martling galloped into town with their new companions. Like most days, there were already a few people waiting for them at their table in front of the tavern.

Horses were tied up at the tavern, and Julian and Martling could see the Chief was already on 'his' bench, napping.

"Can we talk business now, Marshall Crane?" the lead man asked.

"Yes, we can."

"We heard you're picking each member of this posse."

"I am."

"Have you done so yet?"

"I will as soon as my backside touches that chair." Julian pointed.

The man dismounted, walked to the table, grabbed both empty chairs, and threw them down the road. Julian watched, not knowing if he should be amused or angry.

"What'd you do that for?" Martling yelled.

The lead man stepped closer to Julian. "So, Marshall Crane, are you going talk to the men you're going to hire for your posse, right in front of you, or is your mind set on hiring men who aren't going to be a part of your posse?"

"You are either confident in yourself or full of yourself.

I'll give you that. Give me one reason why I should hire you and your men over any of the dozens of qualified men I have interviewed over the past week and probably many more today."

"This Horseman killed your uncle, right?"

"Yes, it did."

"Well, Marshall Crane, I don't give a damn. We can either go together or separately. But either way, I've spent almost two years, not a mere week, putting together my gang, and we're going to hunt down whatever this thing is, one way or another. You're not the only person on this Earth who has a black heart of vengeance for this Horseman of Sleepy Hollow. We're part of your posse, as of now. It killed your uncle? This Headless Horseman of Sleepy Hollow killed my father! That puts me ahead of you in the vengeance line."

Into the Darkness We Ride

"What evil may come."

It never occurred to Julian that there could be anyone else like him out there. The Horseman killed his uncle, but he knew there were others—many others. He never once thought of the families of its other victims. If there was a line for revenge, then others could conceivably have precedence over him.

There was Flynn Shaunessy. The Headless Horseman disappeared a decade ago, but not before adding his father to its long list of victims through the years. Shaunessy told a compelling story. He, too, was spurned to action from a letter, but his was from the victim himself, his father, Finn. The man said it took him half the decade to piece together all the accounts, and trace his unfortunate father's steps— venturing alone, and came to the certainty that his father had fallen prey to the Horseman maybe a month, or even weeks before poor Ichabod Crane.

Julian entered the tavern. The proprietor saw him and immediately walked to him.

"I've concluded my business," Julian announced.

The proprietor smiled. "You have your Super Posse then?"

"I will by noon. Can you keep it quiet until then?"

"Yes, Marshal. I'd leave the chair and table out there and have the Martling boy talk to people for show."

"Good idea."

With Martling doing the day's interviewing, Julian and Baltimore walked to the inn where he had told the gang to settle in for the day.

"You approve?" Julian asked.

Baltimore nodded.

Julian left a message for them at the front desk rather than possibly waking them up. He and Baltimore headed back to the tavern to continue the ruse. There was no sign of the gang even well past noon.

By sundown, Julian, Martling, and Baltimore sat in the raucous tavern for supper and drinks. Most of the people in the tavern, however, were there to spy on them. Who would become the Sleepy Hollow Super Posse to hunt down the Horseman?

The gang walked into the establishment at a quarter past six o'clock. Their leader was Shaunessy. He looked like a lawman himself with his black hat, well-kept clothes, and the way he carried himself. He walked ahead of his men and scanned everyone in the place until he found his target.

"Join us," Julian said when they made their way to the table.

He sat across from Julian. The rest of his men sat at nearby tables.

"What's the verdict Marshal Crane?"

"You're right," Julian answered. "You put together a

team better than I could have dreamed of. I'm keeping the Chief and Martling, and we'll add you and your men."

Shaunessy looked at Baltimore. "Chief?"

"Yes," Baltimore said.

"I've never seen a White Indian before."

"There's quite a few of us."

"Why would Red Indians make a White Indian their chief? That doesn't make any sense."

"It happens when the only able-bodied male left in the tribe is a White Indian. All the Red Indians were killed off by war and disease. We've been fighting Whites for nearly two hundred years—since the 1600s. There's no end to you."

Shaunessy laughed. "Don't look at me. But from what I know of pre-America times, there was a whole lot of killing before the White man ever set foot on this land."

The Chief smiled. "Like I said, we've been fighting Indians for nearly five hundred years. There's no end to us."

Shaunessy laughed again. "How will this work? I'm in charge of my men and they won't listen to any other as their boss."

"Even though I'm the only one who knows where the Horsemen is?"

"And the Marshal has the bounty money?" Martling added.

Shaunessy leaned back.

Martling smirked. "Yes, the bounty money. That's why you want on to our posse."

"Co-leaders," Julian said. "I direct my men, you direct your men. But we acknowledge neither team can accomplish anything without the other. All survivors will get the bounty money. We have a disagreement, then we settle it off to the side away from the men."

Shaunessy nodded. "Co-leaders. Agreed." The men shook hands.

"I want us to get all the men to the barn to devise our plan as a team," Julian said. "Get to know each other over a day or two, and then leave at dawn by the third day."

"Why not leave now? We can get to know each other on the trail."

"We must know the plan before we ride out. We can't be planning and plotting on the way. I've been in these parts a relatively short time and there's always some distraction. The only thing we should have on our minds is hunting down the Horsemen. Believe me when I say, thinking about facing the Horseman is far different than actually facing it."

"I'll get the men together and follow you," Shaunessy said. "But remember we've been waiting eighteen months for this time. We'll wait a day or two, but no more."

"Agreed."

It was not yet the deep of winter, but the morning was freezing. However, there the two Bully Boys were, the largest and meanest of Shaunessy's gang, bare-knuckle brawling without their tops on. The men could almost be twins with broad-shoulders, barrel-chested, and hairy. One of them had a scar down his right cheek giving him the nickname Scar. Droopy-Eye's left eye was perpetually closed. The men entertained themselves outside the barn door by beating on each other and laughing the whole time with mouths of missing teeth.

"They do this all the time?" Julian asked. He stood next

to an equally uncomfortable Shaunessy.

"Either this or they'll beat on one of us. Or worse, go into town and beat up some helpless stranger."

"We can't have this when we ride out."

"It'll stop then. They'll be thinking about how they plan to snatch the Horsemen down from his horse and rip him apart, bone by bone. If it can be done, then they can do it."

"Time to stop their horseplay."

Shaunessy moved to the Bully Boys. "'Nough you two! Let's get started!"

The Bully Boys stopped their brawling, laughing hysterically at each other. The men watching were amused, disgusted, or indifferent.

"I'll introduce my men and Marshal Crane, his."

"And the particular talent which make them worthy of our posse," Julian added.

"What about you Marshal Crane," Scar blurted out as he put on his shirt. "All I heard about you is you accused an innocent man of killing your uncle and ran with your white tail between your legs when you did face this Headless Horseman."

"You heard a lot more than that," Shaunessy defended. "He put down the best men in the town … "

"The best men in this nothing-town means nothing," Scar interrupted.

Julian walked up into his face. "I don't need to explain anything to you. You talk a lot about how you're going to do this, that, and the other to the Horsemen. You will get your chance, but he won't be one of those defenseless townspeople half your size, including women and children, or some lone hapless dog I hear you and your twin like to beat up for fun. Yes, I found out about you, too. Don't worry. You'll get your chance to show how fearless you really are."

Scar grinned at him. "The Headless Horseman will be an Armless and Legless Horseman after we get done with it. Then we'll take it and beat you unconscious with his bones."

"Beat you unconscious with his bones," Droopy-Eye repeated and laughed.

Julian looked at Shaunessy. He walked away from them.

"They can kill anyone or anything with their bare hands," Shaunessy said. "They have awful manners and no one likes them, but they can do what they say."

Julian said nothing else. Shaunessy continued his run-down of his gang.

There was the Austrian. He was a tall, slim man with a long stringy mustache. Strapped on his back was some type of rifle in a sheath. His talent was this special rifle and his proficiency in its use. When asked to display it, he declined in a soft, Austrian accent. All he told them was that its name was 'Girandoni.'

"I only take it from its case when I'm going to kill something," he said.

There was the Scottsman—everyone just called him Scotts. He was a red-haired, stocky man. In his arms at all times, though covered, was a large double-ax. Shaunessy had found him performing in a traveling circus for extra money under the name 'The Deadly Ax-man of Scotland.' He supposedly had several assorted throwing axes inside special pockets of his coat.

Morgan was a fidgety man with a perpetual frown. The man complained about everything, and he was always complaining. There seemed nothing remarkable about him to the eye, except he wore a jacket that was about two sizes too big. Shaunessy vouched for him.

"He can do tremendous gun violence," Shaunessy said. "I've seen him in action and I still can't believe what I saw."

There was a Mexican who had a name no one could pronounce, so everyone called him Wrangler. He wore a variety of lassos over his neck and shoulder. Julian couldn't imagine any man roping something as terrible as the Horseman. The apparition might just drag the poor man directly to Hell, but all would have their chance to use whatever means necessary for the hunt.

Wrangler also had an assortment of stringed throwing weapons Julian and his gang had never heard of or seen before—bolas—three balls interconnected by cords. He demonstrated on one of the men. Scotts ran as fast as he could and Wrangler threw the rope-weapon. Scotts fell to the ground face-first, his legs all tangled up.

"If I throw it hard enough, it can cause much physical damage—even kill a man if it wraps itself around his neck," he said.

The men thought the same thing. The Horseman had no head. The Wrangler might want to modify his attack strategy.

All of Shaunessy's men were impressed by the hand-cannon carried by Martling, even the Bully Boys.

"Finally, someone with a real weapon," Scar said to him.

Martling was not joking about blasting the Horseman to Hell with one shot. They could see the determination in his eyes.

Chief Baltimore said not a word as he pulled a massive bow from the blanket covering the side of his horse and shot two arrows—one at Julian and one at Shaunessy. The two men were caught off-guard, but stood fast. The two arrows embedded themselves in the barn wall inches above each of their heads. The men burst out into laughter.

"He's an Indian, all right!" Scar cackled.

All day the men planned the trip in the center of the barn. Julian frequently referred to an unfolded map on the floor and plotted out their path north.

"Who gets first shot at the thing?" Scar asked.

"It's already decided. Me," Martling replied. "I'll use the hand-cannon on it."

"What if you miss?"

"Don't be insulting. I won't miss."

Scar looked around at the other men. "Who's next after the boy misses?" Droopy-Eye laughed.

"I won't miss!"

Shaunessy ignored the banter. "Morgan, me, and Crane will all fire at it after Hand-cannon Boy. Scotts, Wrangler, and the Chief have at the Horsemen next."

"And when you all miss, Droopy and I will pull it right from its horse and finish it."

Shaunessy continued. "Lastly, the Austrian will empty his rifle into it, if it somehow gets past all of us."

"Yes, if it gets past all of you, it comes down to me," the Austrian said with an accent. "If it gets past me, then we all better get to our horses and ride away as fast as we can."

As they continued talking, they saw a carriage approach with a black horse in tow; the rider looked familiar. Julian watched, but most continued their conversation.

The carriage stopped and a passenger door opened. Julian froze—Brom Bones!

He was wearing hunting clothes and a fur-skinned cap with a fox's tail hanging from the back. Inside the carriage was Katrina, who gave Julian a passing glance. She turned her gaze back to her husband. Brom looked back at her before leaning in to give her a final kiss. He closed the door and looked at her for a moment longer. Her eyes were teary. He walked to the back of the carriage and untied the horse.

"Dutch, get Mrs. Van Brunt home immediately."

"Yes, Mr. Van Brunt." Dutch gave Julian a dirty look before starting the carriage back around.

Brom's favorite horse, Daredevil, was rumored to be a vicious animal, but he was as quiet as a doe in his master's hands. Brom watched the carriage pull away. They could all see Katrina Van Brunt leaning out the window, looking back. When it disappeared out of sight, Brom turned around to face the men.

"Well, look at this," Scar said sarcastically. "Who's this one with the soft, furry cap and the la-de-da frilly clothes?"

Brom walked to him and cocked him on the bridge of the nose. Scar hit the ground with such a noise, everyone froze. The primary Bully Boy looked up in a daze flat on his back.

"I'm Brom Bones, the richest man for a hundred miles around, and the man financing this posse. You disrespect me again and the least of your worries will be the Horseman."

Julian felt his mouth moving even though he didn't want it to. "Mr. Van Brunt, you don't have to see us off. The posse is assembled, ten men, and we'll be off in the morning."

"No, Mr. Crane. The posse is assembled now that I'm here. Eleven men. Did you think I was going to sit here in Sleepy Hollow and wait for one of you to return and give out my money on yours or their say-so? I will be along every bit of the ride, and I expect to be fully satisfied on the matter of the final demise of the Horseman." He pointed down to the still prostrate Scar. "And I'm unilaterally cutting your share in half, you stupid ox, for setting me in a bad mood."

The posse rode out of Sleepy Hollow at dawn the next day.

The Narrow

*"It was indeed the quietest place in the whole world. But I felt
we were being watched."*

It was nearly noon, but the sky had an overcast that more resembled dusk. They were even able to see shooting stars above. The valley and surrounding region around Sleepy Hollow was actually known for the best star gazing in the country.

Even on the third day, when they were more than fifty miles from Sleepy Hollow and the neighboring towns, they could all still feel 'that witching influence' in the air. It was something that Julian thought he imagined when he first rode into the area, but felt vindicated when other members of the posse told him that they felt it too. The bizarre behavior of animals, the feeling of inanimate objects, especially trees, watching you, and …

"But what were they about?" Julian asked.

"I can't say. All I know is the dreams were … disturbing. And they woke me right up," Morgan said. "I can't remember details."

"When did the dreams start?"

Morgan thought for a moment.

"I don't want to talk about it anymore." Morgan had clearly remembered something from the past. "Talk about something else. I'll stay quiet and listen."

Julian wanted to ask him again but let it go.

"Why are his dreams so important?" Martling asked. "Everyone has dreams and nightmares from time to time."

"Men don't have nightmares. Only boys," Scar interjected.

"Keep quiet," Martling snapped at him. He turned back to Julian.

"Because the dreams are more than dreams," Baltimore said to him.

"What do you mean they are more than dreams?" Martling asked.

"It means that it knows."

"What are you talking about, Chief?" Shaunessy asked.

"Knows we're coming," Julian answered for him, a troubled look on his face.

Baltimore nodded to himself. "I'm pleased to see that you decided to be a wise man rather than a brave man."

Scar and Droopy-Eye looked at each other and started chuckling.

"Listen to them," Scar said. "Talking, but saying nothing."

"I know what they say," Wrangler spoke up. "I had the dreams too, and I remember them all."

Julian looked at him.

Wrangler shook his head. "I, too, wish to keep it to myself."

Brom broke his silence. "What are you men trying to do? Talk yourselves out of this? Do you want to turn back?"

"No one is turning back, Mr. Van Brunt," Shaunessy replied. "Not a one of us is turning back—ever. We started this almost two years ago, and that was without your money."

"We shall see. The only one I know who will go straight to the end is Crane. He and I have had previous dealings."

Julian didn't look at him.

"The Headless Horseman killed his uncle, but it killed my father, so I'll be there to the very end myself," Shaunessy added. "You can bet on it."

"What's the motivation for your men then?" Brom asked.

Shaunessy hesitated. "What does it matter? We're here, we're going, and we're going to kill this thing, or die trying."

Julian told them it would take them many days to get to their final destination, without revealing the exact location. There was very little chatter as the men rode. Every one of them wanted the confrontation now. Each man, including Brom with his new rifle, envisioned how they would 'kill' the Horseman with their particular weapon or skill.

For Shaunessy's gang, they had been imagining the final battle for over a year. Julian glanced at Martling. The boy was quiet too, deep in thought about the moment he'd raise his hand-cannon and fire. Martling imagined what the damage would be to the Horseman. He tried to picture it in gruesome detail. Chief Baltimore pretended to be at ease, but he was as nervous as any of them. He pondered about the battle and practiced each of his moves in his mind.

Julian played out the scenarios in his mind: firing his gun at it, his rifle at it, reloading both, again, again, and again. This time he would not be alone in his rematch with the thing. But how does one kill something that is already dead? Someone had killed it before, but here it was, still terrorizing people.

The Bully Boys were back to their loud and crude manners. Scar had long forgotten his knockdown by Brom and joked and smoked tobacco with his partner. He recounted a story of how they had nearly beaten a fat man to death with an equally fat pig. Julian hoped their utter cruelty and inhumanity would carry over to their encounter with the Horseman.

Shaunessy and the Wrangler rode point. Julian rode behind them, with Brom right next to him and Martling right behind. The other men were following in single file. The Austrian and Chief Baltimore took to the rear.

Every so often, Baltimore would stop and wait while the posse continued forward. Moments would pass and he'd reappear. Julian made eye contact and motioned him to the front. Baltimore galloped up to join him and Brom.

"You seem worried about something behind us," Julian said.

"How many are following us?" Brom asked directly.

Baltimore answered, "At least seven close, but I believe it's many more than that."

Julian shook his head. He realized what Brom already knew.

"We need to get them out of here!" Morgan yelled. "They have no business in our business."

"You didn't really think you'd get your posse out of town and none of the men who wanted to join would remain there," Baltimore said.

"We have to lose them," Morgan said.

"Why?" the Chief asked. "Let them follow. The more men, the better for us."

"Just send them all in at the beginning," Scar butted in. "The Horseman will kill them, and we'll kill the Horseman and collect the reward money." The Bully Boys started to crackle.

Julian avoided eye contact with them because he was so disgusted.

"Sounds like a good adjustment to the plan to me," Shaunessy said.

Julian was surprised by his agreement.

"This is business," Shaunessy continued. "They want to follow us without permission, then we have every right to use them as we see fit."

"No," Morgan said. "They just want to get our bounty money. I'm not giving up my share."

"We can't lead people in to get killed by the Horseman," Martling protested.

"Why not?" Shaunessy countered. The Bully Boys grinned with satisfaction that a boss had taken up their side.

"That would be ... wrong," Martling said.

"They're gunmen too, so they know what they're doing. And since none of us are Lazarus, then it would be best if someone else did the dying," Shaunessy added. To Julian, he said, "You got an objection?"

Julian paused. "No."

Martling was surprised. "Changed your mind fast, Marshal Crane. I thought you were a boss too on this posse. Don't fold to their pressure."

"I'll say again," Morgan added. "I'm not sharing my bounty money, just know that."

Julian looked at Martling. "I'm not folding to pressure. They're right. I'm allowed to say another man is right as a boss. We couldn't make them turn back anyway, and it makes no sense spending who knows how many days trying to lose them on the trail. Besides, we get the posse we have now and the posse we would have had if we hadn't met Shaunessy's gang. All of us hunting the Horseman, but only we share the bounty money."

"That's right!" the Bully Boys yelled out.

"That's all I care about," Morgan said.

"And if they get killed?" Martling asked.

"You don't get it, do you?" Julian said. *"We'll all probably get killed.* No one is going to be shielded from the danger on this hunt."

As they moved north, Chief Baltimore was able to count the gunmen following them—fifty-two men in all, but he added that it was likely that more men were following them. They were about five miles back, but as the hours progressed, they got steadily closer. By the time the posse settled to make camp, the other gunmen were less than a half mile behind doing the same.

Wrangler created a rope fence around the horses as Shaunessy and Martling made the fire. Coffee and bread was to be their only supper.

"We should have sentries during the night," the Austrian said as he lay down on his bedroll. "We don't want to wake up to any surprises."

"Are you volunteering?" Shaunessy asked.

"Yes, if you like."

"It's fine. I'll go first," Shaunessy said. "You take

tomorrow night, and we'll change up every night."

Scotts was fast asleep, and Scar threw a rock at him, but the Scotsman didn't move. The Bully Boys laughed. Julian and Shaunessy watched them carefully. Soon, the Bully Boys moved onto something else to occupy their time.

"How quickly can we get there?" Shaunessy asked. "How long did it take you last time?"

"I didn't go direct last time," Julian answered. "But I think it will take us ten days in total. We'll keep a steady pace and not overwork the horses."

"How did you find where it lives?" Brom asked.

Julian hesitated.

Shaunessy said, "Didn't it exclusively inhabit Sleepy Hollow? But you're taking us north."

"The former U.S. Marshal found a way to move it."

Brom perked up. "How?"

"The Marshal?" Shaunessy asked.

"Marshal Damian," Brom told him.

"He found its head," Julian answered.

The men were quiet for a moment.

"What did you say?" Martling was lying on his side.

Julian noticed that everyone in the camp was listening, even Scotts had awoken.

"How did he find that?" Brom asked. "Everyone in the Hollow has looked for it for years. I, myself, dug up half the countryside as a boy."

"I don't know, but he did." Julian sipped the coffee from his tin.

"What happened to the late Marshal?" Brom asked. "The whole story."

"He tried to kill me. I killed him first."

Shaunessy looked at both men. "Why would a marshal

try to kill another marshal?"

Julian answered, "The Marshal was an evil man. Let's just say he was a … "

"Servant," Baltimore interjected. "He was a servant of the Horseman."

Julian nodded. "Yes. He led people to it…killed them. He was going to do the same to me."

"The Marshal did that?" Martling asked, incredulously.

"Don't act surprised," Brom said. "A lot of people in town felt something was suspicious about him."

"Led people to be killed? How many do you think?" Martling asked.

"Who will ever know? But the Horseman disappeared ten years ago. That's a lot of time for a man to do evil things for a thing of evil."

"But I don't understand the head thing. The legend says, if the Horseman finds his head, then he disappears from the natural world. Not that he moves up north," Shaunessy said.

"I know where we're going now," Baltimore said and turned on his side with his back facing them and the fire.

"What?" Martling said. "What do you mean you know where we're going? How?"

"Then the legend is wrong," Julian said.

"Chief, how do you know where we're going?" Shaunessy asked Baltimore.

With his back still turned he said, "The tribe elders told me about the place. It is a land surrounded by storms and deranged animals. It's the only place it could be."

Julian's expression told the men that the Chief did know where they were going.

"Why there?" Shaunessy asked.

Baltimore turned. "Obvious. Something evil happened there."

"Like what?" Morgan asked. "Evil happens all over. Why there?"

"I don't know." Baltimore smiled. "I'm not an Indian."

The Bully Boys laughed. "That's funny," Scar said.

Suddenly, Shaunessy jumped up from the ground. "Who's there?!"

Everyone in the camp turned to see what he was looking at. A man slowly came out of the shadows with a sheepish grin. "Hello. Hello everyone. Uhh…Marshal Crane, sorry to disturb your supper, but … I know you know we're back here. Any chance of us all joining forces."

"Maybe, but keep your distance until we motion for you," Julian answered.

"That's fine, Marshal Crane. I'll let the others know. Thanks Marshal." The man bowed repeatedly and disappeared into the shadows.

"That man could have gotten his head shot off," Shaunessy yelled.

"I wish we had a mean dog with us," Morgan said. "That would teach anybody from sneaking up on us. How long was he there, anyway, listening?"

Julian stood up. "Gentlemen, we have a long day ahead. We need to get our sleep."

He situated himself near the fire. In a few moments, all the other men settled in around the fire to turn in for the night.

Julian leaned over to Shaunessy and whispered, "I know your motivation and you know mine. I want to know how you got these men to follow you when there was no bounty money before."

"Why? They're here."

"We'll talk about it at some point. There will be many days for us to pass the time."

Julian moved to his spot and prepared to sleep. Shaunessy threw a blanket over his back and took out his gun to guard the camp.

Over a hundred men were following them. That was the latest count from Chief Baltimore. There were more stragglers following, but most had caught up to the 'other' posse by night with the dual camp fires as beacons for miles around.

Julian noticed the dark clouds towards the east. He remembered them well, and he gave a glance to Baltimore. They were getting closer. The storm couldn't be more than three hours away.

"Is that it?" Morgan asked. "The clouds you said chased you and that other marshal."

"Yes, but we're going to steer far from it. I believe that the Marshal purposely led me in there to kill me."

Morgan laughed. "Didn't work out as he planned."

Shaunessy and Wrangler led the posse. The other posse followed about a quarter-mile back.

Half the sky seemed crystal clear; the other half was black. In the distance, they could hear low rumbling thunder.

"How will we know we're in this Headless Horseman's domain?" Morgan asked.

"You'll know," Julian said. "We'll all know."

They could see their breath and their horses' as they rode. Each day seemed to get colder than the day before.

Morgan and Scotts said it was because they were getting closer to Canada. But no one really believed that—the cold was unnatural.

Nightfall also seemed to come quicker each day. Once the sun was gone, the riding stopped. Camp was setup and so was the other posse's, a ways back. On the day's ride, they learned that Shaunessy was some kind of big card gambler.

"Or a cheater is what some might call you," Scar chimed in.

"I can't help it if you can't master a simple game of chance." Shaunessy threw down a card and picked up another.

Playing card games was the camp pastime these days. All played except for Scotts, who was always sleeping when not riding, and Morgan, who just liked to watch everyone play.

"Scotts! I thought Scotsmen were exceptional card players," Shaunessy said.

"We are," he said from under his hat. "But I don't see any money there, so it's not worth my time."

"We can add some real money for you," Scar said. "I'll put my own in, since I'll end up winning it all back." Droopy-Eye began to laugh.

"Next time," Scotts said.

It came down to Shaunessy and Brom. Scotts had to sit up to watch the final card play. The men stared at each other.

"We have a saying in my home town of Dublin," Shaunessy said. "You're about to get busted up and left in the gutter with your pants down by your ankles."

The men broke out in laughter; the loudest were, of

course, the Bully Boys.

Brom smiled. "We have a saying in Sleepy Hollow. You're about to have the Horseman reach his skeleton hand up through you and yank your pride, in a nasty mess, right down through your private hole."

The laughter was even louder.

"Two aces." Shaunessy laid his hand down.

"Since I am as close to royalty as any of you will ever get, royal flush."

The men cheered. It was a very long time since any of them had reason for joyous outbursts. Shaunessy smiled as he shook his head.

The men turned in for the night. Wrangler had guard duty. The winds were blowing hard and a couple of times he had to tend to the camp fire. They had picked a spot with heavy tree growth on one side and open plains on the other, where they made a rope fence to keep the horses.

Past the camp, through the trees, the night sky was pitch-black, and not even the stars were visible. Wrangler thought it strange since they could actually see some during the day. There weren't even any sounds of animals, insects, or owls. Nothing was normal about this land. Everything was bizarre; everything hinted at a supernatural danger. They were still days away from the Horseman's home. The shorter days of daylight to ride only added more days to get there.

There was a noticeable movement in the trees within its highest branches. Wrangler looked up. Was it the wind, or maybe birds or squirrels? The rustling continued, getting louder, and the men in the camp began to wake. The rustling was not something in the trees, but seemed to be the very trees themselves, from the topmost branches to the trunks.

A giant mass of darkness rose from them and moved away from the camp. The men were wide-awake as the darkness seemed to have its own form and moved—walking—away. It was gone.

They looked back, and the night sky was as clear as could be—the stars and even a full moon! It was never pitch-black; their view was no longer blocked. The moonlight shone through and the group saw that the tree lined side of the camp was not filled with trees at all. There was only some small brush.

Wrangler said nothing. No one did. The men pretended to be sleeping. And Wrangler pretended nothing was wrong as he continued with his guard duty.

Morgan jumped up as dawn arrived. He walked around in circles, talking to himself in a hushed tone. Other men in the camp began to get up.

"What was that?" Morgan yelled. "Why is everyone pretending they didn't see it? What was that?"

Everyone ignored him as they packed up camp.

"Is anyone going to answer me?"

"Morgan shut up!" Shaunessy yelled.

"Something, something huge was sitting here next to us, and got up in the middle of the night." Morgan marched over to Julian. "This posse is supposed to be after one malevolent thing, not two. Mr. Crane, what was that? There was something huge sitting right next to us."

"We're in the Horseman's domain now," Baltimore said and took his things to his horse.

"Are we now?" Morgan said. He turned back to Julian. "Say something!"

"What do you want me to say? I don't know what it was. We could have been imagining it."

"All of us?"

"That's how it was in Sleepy Hollow years ago," Martling added. "People would see all kinds of things that weren't actually there. They'd all see the same thing."

"You don't believe that any more than I do. It wasn't our imagination. There was something there. What was it?" Morgan asked again.

"We don't know," Julian answered. "And we probably never will. We have one mission and that's the Horseman. Nothing else. If you want to come back here after, and look for other things…"

"Not a chance. I'm done with this, and I'm never coming back to these haunted lands ever again."

"Marshal Crane." Baltimore sat on his horse looking out past the camp.

Julian looked at him.

"We're here."

Julian gave him a perplexed look. "What do you mean? Here, where? I'd say we were another two days ride."

Baltimore shook his head. He pointed. "It's through there. I know of this place. It's called the Narrow. It's like I told you before. Evil things happened here long ago, maybe centuries ago. The Marshal didn't bring the Horseman here. He was lying. The Horseman brought him here. This is its home and always has been. Why it went to Sleepy Hollow, we may never know. Maybe it did get its head shot off there and haunted it for a time because of it. But this—the Narrow—is how we avoid the land of the storms. It is the quickest path to get to its lair. That island you spoke of."

"Who's leading who here?" Shaunessy asked. "I thought Mr. Crane was our posse's guide."

"Are you certain?" Julian asked the Chief.

"Yes."

"Then let's go get him." Julian got to his horse.

One Shall Remain

"We beheld a dark and fearful shape to beset our path!"

They took their first break of the day. The horses were allowed to graze while the men attended to the call of nature, tended to their gear, and took a bite of their rations or a drink of water. The Chief and Scotts were the best of the group at making camp fires, followed by Brom. Scotts took a turn and had a roaring fire in no time at all. They could all see the other posse a mile back, but all their noise and commotion made them sound much closer.

Julian stood alone, brushing his horse, Caleb Williams. Shaunessy approached and Julian glanced at him, then returned to firmly brushing down one side of his horse.

"My father was … a hunter of sorts himself," Shaunessy said.

"Hunter? What kind?"

"He belonged to some professional skeptics' society. My father was in the business of disproving the supernatural. He called himself a book author, but that was only his secondary work. Do you remember Salem, Massachusetts? The witch business?"

Julian nodded.

"My family is related to someone who was killed there in the so-called trials. I think that's what motivated my father. Travel 'round and disprove ghost stories and the like. He was quite fearless in his work."

"He went looking for the Horseman?"

"Yes."

"And found it?"

Shaunessy nodded. "He mailed his journal to me the day he disappeared. I think he knew. He knew he'd never see me or his family again. He never let me look at his journal, not that there was much opportunity once I got grown and moved back to Ireland."

"That's how I got on the trail of my uncle. We got a letter from a Mr. Knickerbocker from Sleepy Hollow."

"We have something else in common then."

"Yes." Julian finished brushing his horse. "Are you going to tell me how you got these men to follow you? I know why we're here. The bounty brought the Chief to me, and Martling is a Sleepy Hollow man. But you had your posse without any bounty, without any reward at all."

Shaunessy hesitated, just as he did the last time Julian asked.

"I was on a ship back to the United States with this old gentleman. Nice man. Reminded me of my father actually, though he didn't look anything like him. We talked for a bit, and he asked me to fetch his bags. I did. But when I walked down the gangplank, I found my own bags had been removed from the ship. The elderly man had told them to do so, apparently before I ever came upon him. I also learned that he had died three days earlier. I had been talking to…a ghost, I suppose. Strangely, he was in a coffin being transported and loaded onto the same ship, at the moment I was standing there on the dock. We opened it and it was him, the old gentleman—clearly dead, clearly the man I had been conversing with for quarter of hour or so, even the same clothes.

"I never did take that ship the States. I had to wait for the next one. While I waited in town, I learned that my original ship had sunk somehow. There were no survivors."

Julian listened closely without moving.

"I think it tried to kill me," Shaunessy added. "I think there is a whole war of good and evil going on around us that we cannot even see with our eyes. It—the Horseman, even from a continent away tried to kill me, and the old gentleman, the ghost, some agent against evil, saved me."

"Do you really believe that?"

"I don't know. But after two years of thinking about it, it's the only explanation I can come up with that makes any sense to me. I need to have answers to things or it gnaws at me and won't let me go."

"How did you get your men for the posse? Such a story wouldn't get me to join you."

"No, but it got them to."

"Because they each have their own inexplicable story." His gaze moved to the other men and he walked to them. Shaunessy watched him, wondering what he was going to do.

"Chief," Julian called out.

Baltimore was smoking his pipe, seated at the fire. He looked up.

"Did you join my posse for the bounty money?"

A smirk appeared on Baltimore's face when he pulled

the pipe from his mouth. "Why?"

"That means no. Why did you join? In fact, you seem to know as much about this Horseman as anyone. More than Martling or Mr. Van Brunt even."

"Why are you asking me this?"

"Did the Horseman try to kill you?"

Baltimore stared at him. The other men in the camp watched the conversation—some of them drew closer.

"I believe so."

"How?"

"I was on a tracking job and a black bird, far up in the sky, dropped a spear on me. If another man hadn't pushed me out of the way, I'm sure I would have been impaled through the top of my skull and killed."

Martling had a shocked expression on his face and stood up. Julian pointed at the boy.

"Your turn. Why did you join my posse?"

"Mr. Crane, I wanted to. The Horseman has terrified my town all my life. I have to stop it. And my father left me the weapon to do it," Martling said defiantly.

"That's not my question. Did anything strange happen? Something you can't explain. What was it that you wouldn't tell me the last time I asked?"

"I don't want to talk about it."

"Tell me."

"You won't believe me."

"Martling, I don't think a man here would deny anything you told us as true."

Martling finally relented and told them about the black snake in the barn on his hand-cannon, and how an inexplicable cough from someone not there certainly saved his life.

"And then you go impale your own self through the foot with a knife!" Scar laughed and Droopy Eye joined in.

Julian ignored the Bully Boys. "Is there more?"

Martling had a pained look on his face. "I don't want to talk about it anymore."

"He's not telling us who the ghost was," Baltimore said.

"Ghosts don't cough," Scar said.

Julian looked at each man—Scotts, the Austrian, Morgan, and Wrangler. Each of them turned away. Julian looked down to ground in thought again.

"Morgan, what happened to you?"

"Leave me alone, Crane."

"It's important."

"All that's important is that I'm here."

"Can't you tell me anything?"

"I can tell you, before it happened, I was a straight-as-an-arrow official for the government, and after it happened, I couldn't hold down a steady job. Now, I'm the fidgety, argumentative, impatient, pitiful man before you."

"You're not that, Morgan," Shaunessy interjected.

"Good of you to say, but I am. I have never been at ease since that day—pushed into a dark, dank hole filled with terrible insects as that tiny, evil woman that pushed me, peered down at me laughing. But I managed one shot, right in her forehead. There you have it, Crane."

Wrangler said quietly, "A possessed steer dove off a cliff. It purposely tried to drag me with it. It waited an entire night for me."

Austrian and Scotts looked at each other, neither wanting to say anything.

"You have to tell," Martling told them.

"A man tried to kill me," the Austrian said. "After I had already shot him dead."

"A…monkey," Scotts said.

"A monkey?" Scar yelled.

"This one was carnivorous and about six-feet tall."

"Nothing like that happened to us," Scar said.

"That man," Droopy interjected.

"Oh yes. There was a man always following us with no horse, but he was always where we were. We were going to wait for him and beat him to death, but we didn't see him anymore. No, we joined Shaunessy's gang because we heard of this Headless Horseman, and we wanted to make him the Armless, Legless, Horseless Horseman."

The Bully Boys laughed.

Julian shook his head. "It sent nothing after me."

"It did," said Brom. "Marshal Damian. You said so yourself."

"But it let me escape," Julian said, more to himself than to the group. "Why?" Julian looked up, angry. "Everyone! Be ready. We're moving out."

"Be ready?" Morgan asked. "Be ready for what? We still have a few days ride to get there."

"It knows we're coming," Julian snapped when he mounted his horse.

"Knows we're coming?" Morgan asked.

"What do you mean?" Scar asked. "It's an animal. It doesn't know anything."

Julian took his pistol from his holster and checked it. "I think it purposely let me escape."

"Why do you think that?" Morgan asked.

"Let's ride," Julian called out.

The opportunity to inspect the Austrian's gun had arrived, even if it was by sight only. He would not allow them to touch it, but they could see the sleek, air rifle. They had never seen such a weapon.

"Can it really shoot that many rounds without reloading?" Martling asked.

The Austrian nodded.

"The rifle of the new century," Shaunessy added.

"If every one of our soldiers had one of these repeating rifles, we would have won the War years earlier," Morgan commented.

"If every one of your soldiers had one of these, you would have defeated everyone years ago," the Austrian said. "And wouldn't have needed the French."

"Don't be stupid," Brom said. "If we would have had them, the British would have too."

"It's an amazing weapon," Shaunessy added. "Just don't miss."

The Austrian said with smile, "I never miss."

They continued heading northwest into the Narrow. As they drew closer, all they could see before them were dark woods and rising mountains. The air was also getting colder.

Baltimore was now on point. He had never been to this land before, but felt he knew it, somehow. It was two small mountain chains with a narrow desolate path between them. It stretched for miles, as far as they could see. The air around them felt strange. It was the same kind of atmosphere that he had experienced a handful of times before; like an omen of a coming tornado.

"You want to wait for the other posse?" Baltimore

asked.

"No," Julian replied.

Baltimore continued on with Julian next, then Shaunessy, Martling, Brom, the Bully Boys, Morgan, Scotts, Wrangler, and the Austrian last. The path was not wide enough for them to ride any other way but single-file.

The dark mountain rock was extremely jagged and the shade from the rocks on either side cut down on the visibility. They noticed that the path wasn't completely barren when they were about two miles in. They saw a massive tree leaning to the left side of the path. Before and around it, the path widened considerably. Sounds of the other posse could be heard behind them, but their focus remained ahead.

When the path opened up near the gargantuan tree, Julian and Shaunessy broke out of the single-file formation to ride alongside Baltimore. Both men had galloped forward when Julian realized Baltimore wasn't there. He glanced back and saw Baltimore had stopped his horse.

There was something about how the Chief was sitting there on his horse with his head tilted back as far as it could, looking to the top of the tree. The lone tree was well over forty-feet and, from its width and appearance, seemed ageless. It blocked half the path. Julian stopped Caleb Williams and also looked to the top of the tree.

Something was up there!

The posse had stopped and stared at the top of the black sentinel tree.

At first, they thought it to be a misshapen part of the tree, a growth that had formed over time, something that looked foreign, but was a natural part of the tree.

Martling cowered down into his saddle when the growth moved.

There was no direct light to see it clearly because of the mountains on either side. All they could do was stare at it until their eyes adjusted to the lack of light. Until then, their minds played vicious tricks on their imaginations—it was a giant bat, it was a giant tree slug, it was a massive nest of hornets.

They realized what it was when it moved again, contorting its head from side to side. It was a horse! It was a horse lying on its folded legs, impossibly attached to a tree more than twenty-five feet in the air.

No one moved nor said a word. They stared, frozen.

Another shape became visible on its back. Something was there but there was no way to see it clearly. The mountain shade and the twisted branches all blocked their view.

Julian slowly reached for his gun and hoped that everyone in the posse had their weapon of choice ready, too.

The 'tree' horse rose on all fours and stood there looking down at them.

The posse could hear the other posse getting closer, and with that more noise and commotion. They all wanted to tell them to 'shut up,' but none of them dared speak or move.

A blur of motion. The goblin horse raced down the side of the tree so fast that none of the men had a chance to react, other than to reflexively duck or jerk back. The Headless Horseman became visible to them all as his horse whipped past like a whirlwind and disappeared down the Narrow; back down the path the men had come.

All they heard were screams, and then a few gunshots. More screams. More shots. Nothing.

Julian turned his horse and raced Caleb Williams back. He could hear others following.

They arrived at the scene. *There was no 'second' posse.*

"My God, where did they go?" Morgan yelled. "Where did they all go? It couldn't have gotten them all. There were almost a hundred men here. Where did they go!"

Baltimore stared at the scattered tracks on the ground. "They ran or rode off."

"All of them?" Morgan asked.

"All of them. Look at the tracks. It did something, probably grabbed one of them and rode off. They shot at it."

"That wouldn't make them all run away," Morgan said. "Someone would be here."

Baltimore kept scanning the ground.

Martling got down from his horse. He quickly got his hand-cannon ready and counted to himself with his eyes closed.

If I were the Horseman, when would be the best instant to attack?

He opened his eyes and turned with his hand-cannon aimed.

The Horseman appeared, barreling towards them!

Martling was shocked, but pulled the trigger and was blasted back by the kick of the weapon.

The Horseman's goblin horse was hit point-blank and screamed. The screaming echoed throughout the entire Narrow and beyond.

The posse gritted their teeth and tried to block out the unnatural sound by covering their ears with their hands.

The Headless Horseman leapt from its back and flew through the air onto the back of Scar!

The man yelled out. His eyes bulged as he frantically tried to pull the thing from his back. The Horseman hit the man on the top of his head once and Scar ran. His running speed was not possible, but they all saw it. In a trail of dust, he disappeared down the Narrow with his new devilish rider.

Droopy-Eyes went hysterical, calling out for his companion, and rode off after them.

"No," Shaunessy yelled. "Come back Droop! Don't follow them!"

Droopy-Eyes was gone.

The Horseman's horse lay on the ground on its stomach. Its four legs stuck out, flailing wildly. Its front hooves scratched the ground like they were hands. Black liquid oozed—surely, it couldn't be blood—then poured out of its side.

"Get away from it! You're standing too close!" Morgan yelled at Martling. The boy had picked himself off the ground, holding his weapon. He jumped back from the creature.

The goblin horse turned its body and reached out at Martling, but the boy was out of reach. The men stared on. It started screaming again. The chilling sound was driving them mad.

Morgan first, then Shaunessy, fired at it.

The goblin horse reached all around with its hooves, which seemed to behave more like hands on arms, not hooves on legs. The mass began to violently convulse. All the men moved further back. There was a flash of light from the mass, and then all there was were bones dissolving into the dirt.

Julian had seen men go through the horrors of war before—blown off limbs, body parts. It wasn't only the Horseman that lost his head in battle. Men found many ways to cope with what they saw, the screams they heard, and what they experienced. But this?

Wrangler sat on his horse and didn't move. He hadn't spoken; he just looked around. The Austrian and Scotts quietly stood next to their horses. They hadn't even tried to get to their weapons.

Morgan stumbled around like he was drunk. "This can't be real," he repeated over and over.

Shaunessy sat on the ground next to his horse with his gun in his hand.

Martling rolled on the ground, holding back tears. "It's my fault," he said, convinced that if he had shot the Horseman directly, rather than its horse, the Bully Boys would still be there.

Brom and Baltimore were the sanest of the bunch. They just watched everyone. Julian held his horse close.

Julian walked over to Brom. "Get on your horse and head back to Sleepy Hollow."

Brom was caught off guard. Anger came over his face. "No one and no…thing ever ran me off in my life. I shall not … "

"Brom!" Julian yelled.

Brom quieted down.

"It's decided. You have to get back on your horse and get back to Sleepy Hollow. If we aren't back in a month," —Julian's voice got low and his face got flush— "that means we are never coming back."

Brom said nothing.

Julian continued, "We are far, far beyond our depth, and I don't know if we can get ourselves up to the level we need to be to destroy this thing. But we have to ensure one of us lives. If we don't make it, one of us has to survive. It has to be you, because if we don't make it, you will have to assemble the next posse to come in here and get it done. Kill the Horseman so it can never kill anyone ever again. It has to get done."

Brom had trouble looking at Julian directly.

"I swear to do everything possible to make sure you never have to come back here again," Julian said.

"I swear to do everything possible to make sure no one else ever has to come back here again," Brom said.

The men shook hands.

The Patch

"Where no man dare show his face!"

Brom had ridden out on Daredevil two hours earlier.

Now they were eight.

"Are we sayin' the Bully Boys are dead?" Morgan asked.

"We're saying that we don't expect to see them again," Julian answered.

"Where do you think the Horseman takes his victims, Marshal?" Scotts asked.

"We're going to find out for ourselves, whether we want to or not."

"What's the plan then?" Morgan asked. "If the Horseman can wipe away a hundred men—it already got two of our men—then what are eight men going to do? Nothing, I say. Nothing at all."

"You can turn back if you want."

"Maybe I will."

"Maybe he'll have company, if he does." Wrangler was far from being soft-spoken this time.

"None of us can leave now," Julian said.

"Why not?" Morgan asked.

Julian stopped. "This is about us. It picked off the second posse. It picked off the Bully Boys. It plans to pick all of us off."

"What about that Brom Bones then?" Morgan asked.

"He never was part of the posse. It was always the ten of us. It wanted us right from the start."

"You don't know what you're talking about," Morgan said, annoyed. "'Wants us.' That's nonsense. It goes after anything in its path."

"But we weren't in its path," Julian answered. "It was waiting for us up on that tree." He glanced at Martling. "Did you ever hear of it doing anything like that ever, in any account of it?"

"No," Martling answered. "But it has done other things."

"Like what?" Morgan asked. "Since you're the resident expert on the Horseman, tell us. What else will it do if we continue after it?"

"Well, its horse that I shot. It disappeared in a flash of fire. That made me think of it. I remember Old Man Brouwer said the Horseman could turn to a skeleton and come at you that way, too. Old Man Brouwer said the Horseman did him like that—threw him in a brook when they neared the old church and jumped away over the tree tops and disappeared in a flash of fire and a clap of thunder."

The men looked at him.

"Turned to a skeleton?" Shaunessy asked. "That's crazy. Why would it change from a horseman to a skeleton? It can run you down with its horse."

"That's the story," Martling said. "That's what I heard.

I didn't say it had to make any sense."

"Morgan, what's wrong?" Shaunessy noticed the look on his face.

"Nothing," he answered.

Julian was also deep in thought.

"What are you thinking?" Baltimore asked him.

"It lives on a tiny island. Its devil's pumpkin patch. Let's not keep it waiting."

The night fell and they sat stationed with their backs to the fire. No one could sleep.

"Look," Baltimore pointed into the distance to another couple of campfires.

"Who cares?" Morgan snapped.

"We should see who it is. It could be survivors from the second posse."

"If I were them, I'd do the same thing we're going to do—shoot anything that comes out of the woods," Shaunessy cautioned.

Baltimore stood up. "I'll go."

"You can't go out there by yourself," Julian said.

"I think the Horseman is done with us for tonight. Haven't any of you noticed that? The Horseman is supposed to attack victims at night, but here all the attacks have been by day."

"Baltimore, you think too much," Shaunessy said. "It is as it is."

"It all means something, though. If they are survivors from the second posse, then we need to know exactly what happened. The more we know, the better our chances of defeating this thing. Or at least living through it, ourselves."

"I wouldn't give a spit for any of us surviving to week's end," Morgan added.

There were only five men sitting and staring at their campfire with almost zombie-like expressions. They had only two horses between them.

"No one draw their gun," a voice said. "It's Baltimore from the main posse."

All of the men stood up.

"Baltimore?" one said. "Chief Baltimore? Are you the only one that survived?"

Baltimore came out in the light. "We lost two men."

"Then that would make you fortunate," another man said.

"Come back to our camp and tell us what happened."

The men were nervous. They looked at each other and none of them moved.

"Just to tell us the story," Baltimore continued. "At day break, I'll point you to the right path out of here to avoid the Narrow."

"That thing kills you in the day," a man said. "I thought it only came out at night."

"Come back to our camp."

The five men were treated like royalty. They were situated in front of the large fire and given fresh coffee, while the posse eagerly waited for their account.

"You might as well say we only have one horse," a man said. "The second one is injured. Doubt we could get even ten miles a day out of him."

"Get back to the first town," Baltimore said. "At least you can get fresh supplies and rest. You can leave from there when you're ready."

"Tell us what happened," Morgan asked impatiently. "What happened to everyone?"

"That Headless Horseman happened," the man said. "We were all riding into that trail between the two mountain sides and … We didn't know what was happening."

"But you shot at it," Morgan said.

The man seemed agitated. "Shot at it. It didn't care about us, and our bullets were nothing to it. It flew past us. That's how fast it was riding. It snatched up one man — *horse and all!* It was nothing we had ever seen before. It disappeared down the trail. The man was screaming; we were screaming. The man's horse was kicking all around, but the Horseman never let loose its grip. There was nothing we could do. Men just up and rode off for dear life."

"I don't understand. Snatched up the man and his horse?" Shaunessy asked. "You mean he grabbed the man and the horse ran away."

The man stood up. "No, mister. The Horseman's horse ran down our three men on point, trampled them to death, and then the Horseman grabbed the horse of the next man by its neck and carried it off with the rider pinned between them. You never saw anything like it in your life. It was chaos everywhere.

"Then the Horseman came back around without that man and his horse. He was coming for more victims. Men shot at him but nothing. Men ran or rode away as fast as they could. All we could do was try to get past it and pray it would leave us be so we could escape.

"We had assembled about a half-mile away to plan what to do, and then it came again! It hit another man in the head with one of those pumpkins. I'm tellin' you, it broke the man's neck and his head flopped down to the side of his shoulder. Killed him dead. Everyone scattered in every direction. All we saw was the Horseman chasing men. We ran in any direction we could."

"When we got to the site, there were plenty of tracks," Morgan said, "but we didn't see no bodies."

"It killed them," another man said. "Killed them dead and they were all lying on the ground. So if you got there and there were no bodies, the Horseman took 'em." He looked right at Julian. "No man can kill this thing."

At daybreak, the five men of the second posse hobbled off back south. The posse watched them go, wondering if the best they could hope for, assuming they could survive death, was a similar fate; defeated, demoralized, and forever haunted by the experience.

High mountain peaks menacingly stood in the distance, and they could see a great body of water in the distance to the left of it. Baltimore told them that it was Lake Ontario to the left, and Lake George was to the right. They were moving closer to Canada, with the New York-Vermont border to the East.

Above, the skies were thick with circling black carrion birds. The men looked up at them from time to time as they rode through the land; the soil got damper with each horse's step. All around looked more like swamp land, and ahead, the woods were becoming thicker, except for the one path they followed. There were ponds and small brooks everywhere they could see.

"Why are all these vulture birds everywhere? There's nothing!" Morgan yelled out. "The Horsemen didn't leave nothing, so fly someplace else!"

Baltimore turned to him. "The birds are waiting for us."

Morgan looked up. The birds were indeed following them.

The stillness of the land was increasingly interrupted by the call of bullfrogs. They could not see the animals anywhere, but their twangs seemed everywhere. As they continued ever closer to the Canadian border, Julian peered through his telescope.

"That's it," he said.

It was the isle that he had run from for his dear life months before. As he remembered, a mist hung over it. The higher it went, the thicker it was, but he saw nothing on the islet glowing like the last time. He turned his gaze to the bridge, which still had its damage—the shattered beams on the right side from impact of the Horseman's deadly pumpkin missile.

They sat on their horses, watching from the ridge. It sloped down rapidly and was a wide-open plain past the bridge, across the water, and to the tiny island.

Shaunessy said, "Let's just storm the little island. No more nice and slow. Attack it all out."

Julian glanced at him. "That's as good a plan as any."

The posse trotted to the bridge and were about to start across the bridge.

On the other side of the fifteen foot-long bridge, they could barely perceive something in the mist and darkness. It was huge and it was waiting, without a stir. The Headless Horseman sat on its new horse. The horse was as black and menacing as the last one.

The men stopped in their tracks. Their skins crawled with fear. Caleb Williams was especially agitated, and

Julian did his best to keep him calm. All the men's horses were starting to spook.

"It's not moving," Scotts said. "Why? What do we do?"

"We do what we came to do," Julian said.

"Oh my…" Shaunessy began to yell out.

The Horseman's new steed set a hoof on the bridge, causing an echo. They watched it closely; practically holding their breaths, so as to not make a sound. The horse! *It had a scar down its right cheek.* The sight of it bound their stomachs in knots.

"It can't be," Shaunessy said.

"Why not?" Baltimore said. "The witch-hunters of my tribe said witches could change a man into any animal."

"It's supposed to be into frogs and bats and wolves."

"Any animal," Baltimore said.

"Martling, please shoot the Horseman this time," Shaunessy commanded. "Put a hole in its chest."

"That's exactly what I intend to do."

"Come on Horseman!" Morgan yelled. "This is what all of us have been waiting for! You and us!"

"Don't do that," Wrangler called out.

"Why?" Morgan said. "What's it going to do? Try to kill us?"

The men watched it. But the Horseman didn't move.

"What's it waiting for?" Morgan asked.

"It attacks when you run," Julian said. "None of us are scared of it anymore."

"Of course we are," Wrangler said. "All of us are scared."

"Martling?" Julian asked. "Are you ready?"

"I'm ready."

"All of us go on the count of three. When we start, we

take it to the end. Earn our bounty money right now."

"What do we bring back as proof?" Morgan asked. "It has no head, so we can't bring back its head."

"I say we bring back that right arm that it likes to throw those devilish pumpkins with," Shaunessy said.

"And likes to grab people with," Morgan said.

"It's settled then," Julian said. "One. Two. Three!"

The men charged at the thing across the bridge, but there was no movement from it. Martling started to panic. They had no plan for it standing there for them to run full speed into its new goblin horse.

The horse moved. The Horseman rode forward with the intensity and speed of a hurricane wind.

Martling fired his hand cannon into the Horseman. The boy was knocked back in his saddle, but held his balance.

Both Julian and Shaunessy fired once into the Horseman's chest.

The Horseman rode right through them. Martling and his horse were knocked completely off the bridge. Shaunessy was thrown into Julian, and Julian was thrown from his horse into the water, too. Shaunessy crashed down onto the bridge, hard.

Scotts had already jumped off his horse and threw one ax after another into the Horseman's body. When it was right upon him, he pulled his large double-ax from his coat and swung with all his might. The ax embedded itself into the Horseman's upper torso and dragged the Scotsman along wildly. The goblin horse swung its head to the side and bit the man's forearm. Scotts yelled out as he released the ax and fell hard onto the bridge.

Baltimore managed one arrow shot, then another. Morgan emptied gun after gun at the Horseman.

The Austrian had already stopped his horse and jumped down. He was ready. Every previous night he primed the air rifle's reservoirs by hand pump, stroke after stroke. The men had never seen a repeater-rifle at work but doubted anyone could have done better. The Austrian emptied shot after shot, the first dozen, and then the second dozen, into the back of the fleeing Horseman. His Girandoni hardly made a sound, and there was no gun smoke. But they could see that none of his shots had missed their inhuman target.

The Austrian got off another three shots as something flew through the air over his head. The Wrangler had thrown another bolas at the Horseman as he chased it on his horse. The first rope weapon wrapped itself around the torso of the Horseman. The second caught in its goblin horse's hind legs.

But nothing stopped the forward momentum of the Horseman as it rode up the slope and disappeared over the ridge.

Julian climbed out of the water and onto the bridge.

"Get ready!" he yelled. "It will come around again."

"Help!" Martling held onto his horse and was fighting something in the water.

"What is it?" Shaunessy yelled.

"Something's in the water!"

Martling kept fighting and his horse began panicking.

There was a shot. Julian lowered his gun. A dark shape floated away from Martling. It bobbed up once and they saw for a second what looked like the shrunken face of Droopy-Eye, but the thing was some kind of fish. The giant fish sunk into the depths of the water and disappeared.

"What was that?" Morgan yelled. "Was that a fish?"

"Martling, get out of the water!" Shaunessy yelled.

"Shaunessy, cover me if the Horseman comes around again," Julian yelled as he got down on one knee and quickly began to reload again."

"Watch out!"

Wrangler's voice yelled out and they had only a few seconds to look in his direction to see not the Horseman coming at them again, but a pumpkin projectile.

The Austrian dove off the bridge to avoid it. Others did the same. The pumpkin hit Caleb Williams, picking the horse off the ground, and sent him hurtling into Julian. Both were knocked off the bridge and splashed into the water.

"Crane!" Shaunessy ran to the edge of the bridge.

The Horseman came again. Axes, arrows, and bullet holes in its body were no matter. It rode with the same full-speed, from the ridge to them on the bridge.

Martling yelled, "Kill its horse! We did it before, we can do it now!"

The Austrian emptied his gun into the head of Horseman's steed—his final shots. The Horseman veered from its path to them on the bridge and, instead, raced out of sight along the edge of the riverbank.

Julian coughed water from his lungs and realized he was holding onto the roots of the pumpkins that infested the islet, protruding through the soil into the water. He looked up, and there was Caleb Williams walking erratically on the unholy ground.

He quickly crawled up onto the tiny island, and then walked to his horse. He looked into Caleb Williams's eyes, and something was off; the eyes weren't focusing. Julian hesitated but ran his hand on the other side of his horse's body—it was wet to the touch. He prayed it was just the water, but looked at his hand—blood. Julian came around the side of his horse. The body was crushed—caved in.

"Oh no. Hang on boy. Only a little while longer and we'll finish this."

"Where's Crane?" Morgan yelled.

"I don't know," Shaunessy answered. "Anyone see him?"

"There he is," Scotts yelled out.

They could see Julian standing on the edge of the island. He waved at them to come across the bridge.

"Did you see that?" Martling asked. "We can't hurt it, but we can hurt its horse."

"We need to hurt it," Morgan yelled. "We need to kill it, not its horse."

"How?" the Austrian asked. "Look what we did to it and nothing. We only got its horse to change its path at the last moment, but it will be back."

As the rest of the posse moved quickly across the bridge, Julian was angry with himself for not remembering sooner. Maybe the Horseman wanted him to forget.

Julian yelled to them, "We kill it by killing everything around it." He looked around at the islet. "We kill it by killing the things it cares about. It comes here, and it uses these pumpkins. When I was here the last time, the pumpkins were actually glowing. This is the secret to its power. We kill its lair—this devilish pumpkin patch island."

"How do we do that?" Shaunessy asked. "We hit it

with everything we got it, and it acted as if we did nothing."

"But we hurt its horse," Martling said again. "And we killed the last one."

"And how did that work out for us?" Morgan asked.

"All we did is slow it down," Shaunessy said. "We must stop it."

"The key is this island," Julian said. "Why here? Why this island? I doubt it picked it because it's covered with pumpkins. Chief, you said it yourself. This ground is evil. We destroy it, and we destroy the Horseman."

"These are not pumpkins," Baltimore said.

The men looked at him for a moment. They slowly peered down at the pumpkins at their feet. A faint mist hovered right above the ground, but they could see the soil—matted foliage with larva crawling everywhere. So many insects could only mean one thing. There had to be something dead for them to feast on—a lot of dead things.

Pumpkins of all sizes covered the island, from melon-shaped to as small as a grape; but the larger ones—what they thought were pumpkins—*were mummified heads*. The shock of it made the men back away, back towards the bridge, except for Julian.

Julian stood still and stared with sadness. The silhouette was unmistakable. Ten feet away he saw the head on a mound. It was the head of his dear uncle Ichabod Crane! He had found his long lost uncle. It had an expression of horror forever frozen on his face. The skin was pale-white. The eyes were devoid of pupils; pure-white. The teeth were black.

He stared at what amounted to his uncle's final gravesite. Who knew where his body was? Or where any of these men's bodies were?

"Sorry, Mr. Crane." Martling stood beside him. "Ichabod didn't deserve this fate. None of them did."

Shaunessy looked at each head while boiling with rage. He moved around frantically and squinting his eyes through the mist.

Julian grabbed him and shook his head. "Remember your father as he was, not this."

"You're right," Shaunessy said and stopped looking at the heads.

"They should all be remembered for what they were before," Julian said.

"Julian, this is…far beyond us," Shaunessy said. "How many dead men must be buried on this island cemetery? We have to accept that we can't beat this thing. We need to go. Get out of here while we still can. Maybe we can make it out alive."

"Where is it?" Julian asked. "Why isn't it here?"

None of the men knew what to say.

"Does that not seem peculiar?" he continued. "We're practically helpless. It could attack us and we'd be defenseless. We're distraught, tired, bullets mostly gone, and weapons gone. It could wipe us out with one pass, but it is nowhere to be seen. Why?"

The men looked all around. The island, the bridge, past the bridge, and across the water. Julian was right. The Headless Horseman had not returned to finish them off. Why indeed?

"I know why." Julian marched away from them.

"What are you doing, Crane?" Morgan asked.

Julian stopped. "I was right. This devilish pumpkin patch island is the center of its evil power. That's why it isn't here. It can't hurt us here."

"How do you know that?" Shaunessy asked.

"You know no such thing," Morgan added. "It's watching us, laughing, however a headless thing can laugh, but that's what it's doing."

Julian looked at them directly. "Let's not debate it. You asked me a question before. Ever seen a wildfire? We're going to burn this island straight to Hell. Everything!"

"It's too damp," Scotts said looking around at the ground. "We'll never make it burn."

"We can and we will!"

"You want a wildfire?" Baltimore asked.

"The biggest one that's ever been in these parts. I don't care if we have to burn all of northern New York, all of Canada, as long as this island burns to the bottom of the riverbed."

"We can't do it here," Baltimore said.

"If Crane is right, and we leave the island, then the Horseman will attack us," Morgan said.

"Chief, you take the men with you," Julian directed. "I'll stay here. I'll see how much I can burn right now. It can't be in two places at once, as far as we know, so I'll keep it here. Go."

"How do you know it will come for you and not us?" Baltimore asked.

"I'm about to desecrate its base of evil. It will want me," Julian answered.

Baltimore led the posse to their horses and they started across the bridge. He watched them disappear over the ridge.

He looked over to his horse. Caleb Williams was lying on its side, breathing shallowly. Julian's face was flush with deep sadness.

"Caleb Williams, let's show this Horseman what it's like to lose something dear."

A shot echoed across the Horseman's putrid island.

There was nothing left to do. Caleb Williams was a better horse than any man could have ever asked for. He could not be left to suffer. Julian knelt down to pat his horse as he set his gun on the ground. The water had claimed his holster and all his ammunition when they were thrown in by the Horseman's pumpkin missile. There was only that final bullet in his gun. The men would have said he was a fool for wasting it on the horse rather than defend his life but, for Julian, it was the only sensible thing a man could do.

The island was the final resting place for both his uncle and his horse.

Julian got all his matches from the saddlebag on his horse. He glanced up and noticed the perpetual mist was growing in thickness. The path and view to the bridge was already obstructed. Like most of the inanimate things in these lands, the mist seems to be willfully creeping to him.

He had to get to higher ground, and that meant the center of the island. His mouth hung slightly open as he tilted his head back.

How did we not see it before?

The center of the island had a tree that looked very much like the Major Andre's tree of Sleepy Hollow, but much larger, much taller, and it was not alone. All around it were many black, twisted trees huddled tightly against it. The trees went so far into the sky they had to be more than fifty feet. The misty haze was both near the ground and hanging over the island to block the giants from the view of all.

Julian wasn't so sure about moving to the center of the isle anymore. He suddenly had a feeling. What waited for him in those trees? Maybe the trees themselves might do something to him.

How long would it be before the posse returned for the final attack? He'd never felt so lonely and helpless.

Julian decided to move anyway. Not to the exact center of the island trees, but away from the stalking mist. He could see the mist growing in size all around the island.

Howls pierced the air.

Julian saw them. From across the isle, on the riverbank, maybe fifteen feet away, a pack of coyotes watched him with glistening eyes and snarling. With their blackened fur, were they the same ones who made a meal of the late Marshal? He heard the familiar cawing of birds. The black vultures were also nearby, arriving for what they hoped would be a fresh corpse, or more than one. Julian remembered! He looked to his feet and winced as he avoided the insect-infested soil. The domain of the maggots circled each mummified head, but every other crawling thing covered everywhere else on the island. He could hear the sounds of frogs, and now the unmistakable hissing of snakes. The Horseman had summoned not just the mist, but every possessed animal, fowl, and insect for him.

He moved closer to the trees and suspected that this was the Horseman's ultimate plot. He had to keep calm. He had to wait for his comrades.

The blackened, gnarled pine trees stood before him. If that was where the Horseman wanted him to go, why? What was there? Julian fixed his eyes on them and didn't blink. He would not move from his spot, even as the mist began to reach him.

When blackness stands in front of blackness, is it possible to perceive their distinctiveness?

Julian sensed there was something else amongst the black trees facing him. The sounds of the crazed animals around him grew in intensity. The mist closed in around him. Julian knew he was not alone.

A fire arrow lit up the darkened sky as it sailed down and landed in the top of a nearby mummified head.

Julian could now see the Horseman. It stood before the trees with a twisted, black battle-ax in its right hand. There were no more bullets for Julian's gun. All he could do was watch the thing, but there was no fear in his body. Julian felt the urge to do what the Bully Boys bragged they would do to it — snatch it up and beat it to death. If it came to it that is exactly what he would attempt to do.

Another fire arrow landed on the island, followed by another.

A rolling growl grew in the pit of the Horseman's stomach and a psychotic yell erupted from the stump where its head once sat. It raised its arms, dropping the ax to the ground, and continued its maddened reaction to the sight of the fire arrows, now in steady succession, dotting the entire isle.

As the growing spots of fire multiplied, with each one growing in size, the mist magically began to roll away from the island. There were no animal sounds anymore. The only sound was from the crazed Horseman.

Its cries stopped. The Horseman walked away from Julian and reached down to pick up one of the mummified heads.

"Oh God, no." Julian's mouth hung open.

The Horseman turned around to face him with Ichabod's head upon his neck stump.

Julian walked back slowly in a state of disbelief and horror as he watched. The Horseman reached down again with both hands. It plucked the human heads from the ground, and stuck them—the decay and moisture made them the texture of natural glue—to Ichabod's head, and then to the others. As the fire arrows continue to rain down, the Horseman was in a frenzied state as it hurried along at an accelerated pace, its body stooped, grabbing heads and attaching them to the others on its shoulders.

Parts of the island were in full blaze as Julian looked for a place to run.

"Marshal Crane!"

Julian recognized Martling's voice and turned to run away to him.

"I'm here!"

He saw them around the bridge. Baltimore was shooting the fire arrows like a tireless automaton. The other members of the posse dipped arrows into a nearby campfire until the arrowhead was fully ablaze and handed them to him. Julian ran across the bridge to them and felt his legs give out. He crashed to the ground, but quickly sat up, propping his body up with one arm to let them know he was okay. He got to his feet.

They watched as half the isle was raging with fire.

"What is that?" Morgan asked.

It was the only time Baltimore stopped his arrow-shooting. He, too, couldn't believe what he saw on the isle in front of him. The form disappeared behind the smoke of the fire.

"Don't stop shooting," Julian said. "Burn the island. Burn it all."

Baltimore grabbed another arrow and began to shoot again.

"Can you reach the trees?" Julian asked.

Baltimore stopped and gave him a look. "Trees?" The Chief moved closer to the river bank, stared, and then saw them. He aimed the bow at a higher angle, pulled the string back further, and let the arrow go. Each one hit their mark.

"YOU..."

It was not one voice, but the sound of many talking at the same time. Each man felt a chill and had to fight the impulse to run. Baltimore began shooting again at the trees. Some of the outer trees were already on fire, but the largest one in the center was not.

With the light of the fire from the island and some of the trees, they could see it.

"...CANNOT DESTROY ME!"

The Horseman was no longer headless. It had Ichabod's head. It had the heads of dozens and dozens of men, creating a sick balloon-like mass on its shoulders. Each of the heads were talking in unison.

The Horseman, with all its heads, climbed up the giant, gnarled black tree in the center. The tree was not burning, despite the arrows Baltimore had already shot at it.

"YOU CANNOT DESTROY ME!" The heads began to laugh as one.

"Shut it up!" Martling cried.

"Chief, shoot it. Shoot it, not the tree," Morgan yelled.

"I'm trying," Baltimore said back with a look of distress. "The arrows can reach, but they're not."

"It's time to finish this," Shaunessy said defiantly. "Marshal Crane, you're with me."

Shaunessy mounted his horse and Julian did not have to say anything.

"Marshal Crane, take my horse," Martling said.

Julian got up on the horse and patted its side. "You have a plan?"

"I have something better."

Julian took the gun from his holster. "I need bullets, too."

The Horseman's many voices continued to echo across the tiny island, now yelling and laughing in some unknown language.

Shaunessy and Julian raced to the trees. Most of the island was ablaze now, but the Horseman had climbed to the very top of the most massive tree, fifty-five feet up. From a distance, it looked like a giant sphere sat there.

They dismounted. Shaunessy unfastened one of the saddlebags from his horse and shooed the horse back the way they came. The fire was closing in. They had very little time. From the corner of his eye, Julian saw something moving on the island.

"Go!" Julian yelled. "Do what it is you're going to do."

Shaunessy saw the goblin horse too, galloping to them. He ran into the trees, and Julian stood his ground with a gun in each hand. Julian wished he had his tomahawk as he aimed at the hell-horse. Instead, it veered off and rushed past him.

Shaunessy!

Julian ran after it as fast as he could. The space between the trees, vines, and brush was so tight that most of the light of the fire was blocked out. He pulled himself through and saw the goblin horse, not climbing but slowly clawing up the massive main tree with its strange, sharpened hooves. It was only seven feet up, but Julian remembered the speed of the last goblin horse.

Shaunessy was higher up the tree with his saddlebag hanging over his back, climbing fast after the Horseman. Julian never saw a man climb so fast. The Irishman had to be allowed to succeed.

Julian marched, with sheer determination and hate, to the hell-horse and fired both guns simultaneously at its head. The creature fell from the tree.

Blackness.

Julian slowly gained consciousness and heard laughing. The pain in his chest was crippling. The goblin horse had instinctively kicked him as soon as its hind legs touched ground, and Julian was thrown at least six feet back. It resumed crawling—after him!

Julian could barely breathe and was unable to move, no matter how much he tried. The horse's face came closer with its scar under one pitch-black eye. Julian laid his head back down to the ground and closed his eyes.

Looks like I will join both my dear uncle and dear horse this day.

He opened his eyes and saw a fizzling glow descend from the air at the goblin horse. It landed. The explosion showered Julian with debris and dirt. He opened his eyes again and looked around. The hell-horse was gone. He noticed another fizzling glow high up in the tree. One flew towards the Horseman's perch, and then another. Then he saw Shaunessy jump from the tree and fall.

The double explosions lit up the sky.

"NO!" The many screaming voices echoed across the

entire island.

The massive black tree shattered in two and the Horseman, and all his heads, fell to Earth in a ball of fire!

After

The Diary of Hans Van Ripper

(Edited a bit by Diedrich Knickerbocker because I cannot write worth a damn)

As I reflect upon this past year, I am both overjoyed and saddened. The return of Sleepy Hollow's Super Posse last year was marked by weeks of celebration. Every last member of the posse was made rich by Mr. Van Brunt, and Mr. De Graaf made that day of their return an honorary holiday.

Ichabod Crane did get his justice, and I was happy to have lived to see it, but he was still gone from this world long before his proper time.

The men of the posse were all cheers and laughter at the endless festivities in their honor, but I knew that part of it was for appearance's sake. The men survived something horrific, and all showed physical signs of distress. All of them had prematurely aged; even young Martling had gray hairs now, and they felt, despite surviving, that their full thread of life may have been shortened by the event.

I later learned that all of them, especially Shaunessy and Julian, suffered from many sleepless nights, and when they could sleep, they were plagued by nightmares. The encounter would remain with each of them for all the days of their lives.

Julian did fully recount every moment of their quest to me and Diedrich; and the ultimate banishment to Hell of the former supreme specter of Sleepy Hollow. The Headless Horseman was no more.

In time, the celebrations were over and everyone continued on with their lives.

Julian spent a final week with me before he finally got the courage to purchase a new horse, which he proudly named Lil' Caleb, a splendid looking mare. He saddled up and headed south where he said he had already secured a job working for, no less than, the President of the United States, Mr. Jefferson. He arrived there as the U.S. Capital was being moved from Philadelphia and settling in at its new home in Washington DC. Soon after, though, and who could blame him for not wanting to be a part of such an adventure, he joined the President's Great Lewis and Clark Expedition to find a northwest passage to the Pacific. With him went, none other than, fellow Super Posse compatriot, the Austrian, with that special repeating air-rifle of his.

Young Martling, the Hollow's own, became our duly appointed sheriff. I know we have Julian to thank for that. Martling left after the Horseman as boy, but came back a man. We surely needed him after learning the truth of the last marshal, and knowing we could never get Marshal Julian to stay on. Soon, Tarry Town will be a city with many more newcomers to the region.

Morgan and Wrangler took their bounty reward and headed south, but then I heard they both joined America's new navy and were off to Africa! They went aboard the USS Enterprise, and traveled to Tripoli and Algiers, places neither I nor anyone else has ever heard of, in the War against the Barbary States. I say, wherever and whoever they are. They just needed to be some place with lots of people around and where they had never been before.

We figured Shaunessy would return to China, since it was there he discovered those fireball bombs that ultimately sent the Horseman to its end in a fiery blaze. Or maybe join a traveling circus like Scotts was in, since, after dispatching the Horseman, he managed to jump through the air from one tree at forty-feet to another twenty-feet below to save his life; no circus performer I know could have done better. Instead, he went back to Ireland, which was funny since all the Scottish and Irish seemed to be going in the opposite direction, but he seemed to have his mind fixed on politics. Maybe he spent too much time around Julian.

Scotts didn't follow him. I was told he ended up in Massachusetts to open a fancy pub with his bounty money and sent for his rather large family from Scotland to join him.

Chief Baltimore had the funniest story of the lot. The French brought an end to their own country's bloody revolution, and then decided to make war on everyone else in Europe. But he was undeterred from getting passage on the fastest ship to England, determined to get the title of Lord, Duke, or some such royal nonsense. Indian Royalty is what he wanted to be with his new money.

And Mr. Van Brunt, who was the patron of our Super Posse? Well, he and Katrina welcomed twins into the world.

The Hollow? With so many people moving into the Tappan Zee, we needed another schoolhouse. We rebuilt Ichabod's school over the decaying wreck of the old and named it after Ichabod. I could almost see his grinning, big-eared face from the clouds looking down on us. This project was a parting gift, courtesy of his nephew, Julian.

As for us, Knickerbocker and me, we went on our own journey when everyone else had moved on with life. We rode clear to that island of the Horseman's demise, which the posse described fully as a 'devilish pumpkin patch.' Knickerbocker and me named it the Devil's Patch. We found it was as malevolent a land as the posse had described, even without its Headless master. It was not really an island, tiny or otherwise, at all. It was more like volumes of cursed soil was purposely dropped down high from the skies until, what was not absorbed by the marsh, became the Patch. Maybe there was an original island there long ago. The giant trees that the posse described— only a few remained as broken, bent, and burnt masses— must have been there for centuries.

We always felt uneasy about what Julian had told us about Marshal Damian's servitude to the Horseman or what Chief Baltimore added to the story. The Horseman had some perverse sway over the Marshal, and he over it. But there was something more to their unholy alliance. If the Horseman had its head, why would it continue with its nightly quest for its head, or have the Marshal supply it with victims to take their heads? Its last act to escape the

Super Posse was to gather up all the heads of its victims from its island base. Why would it do that it if had its own?

We checked that land, every spot. Nothing was left but burnt soil, but we checked anyhow. On the third day, we found it. A metal box wrapped in rusted chains secured by a large lock of black metal. It was buried in front of the bridge on the island-side. With all the pumpkins gone, the trees gone, and their roots gone, the entire isle was beginning to wash away. We figured in a few years there would be nothing left of the minuscule island.

It took us days to open the metal box. Despite its good condition, it was ancient, and neither one of us was certain that it was even from the Americas originally. When we did open it, somehow, we weren't at all surprised by what was inside. An atmosphere of such a stink sprung from it that we were almost overcome by a state nauseous sick. We had to hold our breath or we would have fainted cold, or worse.

Inside was the Headless Horseman's head. The pale, shriveled, bloodless thing glared at us. We noticed the faded symbols on the lock and suspected that some kind of ancient spell kept it from the Horseman's grasp. Knickerbocker and me knew that the Legend of Sleepy Hollow must come to an end, as all evil things must.

All I could think of was poor Ichabod, my poor Gunpowder, and all the innocent souls that had been taken from this world before their time. We chopped it up, burned it, and scattered every piece of charred flesh, bone and ash, into the Atlantic Ocean—we made a separate trip for that.

We told no one of this whole affair. The posse did their

part. It was someone else's turn to put the final nail in the coffin, as they say.

Knickerbocker felt especially strong about this responsibility. I never did tell Julian. And we never shall tell any living soul of our part. The Legend of Sleepy Hollow, that foul murderer of Ichabod Crane, is dead.

Now the story is over.

Thank you for reading!

Dear Reader,

I hope you enjoyed *The Devil's Patch*.

Can You Write Me a Review?

If you enjoyed *The Devil's Patch* (*Sleepy Hollow Horrors, Book 2*), I'd greatly appreciate a review on one or more of the following sites:

Reviews are the best way for readers to discover good books. My writer's motto is simple: "Readers Rule!" Thanks so much.

Always writing,

Austin Dragon

ABOUT THE AUTHOR

Austin Dragon is the author of the *After Eden* **Series**, including the *After Eden: Tek-Fall* mini-series, the classic *Sleepy Hollow Horrors*, and the upcoming cyberpunk detective series, *Liquid Cool*. He is a native New Yorker, but has called Los Angeles, California home for the last twenty years. Words to describe him, in no particular order: U.S. Army; English teacher; one-time resident of Paris; political junkie; movie buff; campaign manager and staffer of presidential and gubernatorial campaigns; Fortune 500 corporate recruiter; renaissance man; dreamer.

He is currently working on new books and series in mystery, fantasy, YA dystopia, classic horror, and more science fiction!